VAMPIRE

STORYTELLERS COMPANION ™

BY CLAYTON OLIVER

CREDITS

Author: Clayton Oliver

Additional Material: Justin Achilli

Developer: Justin Achilli

Editor: Cynthia Summers

Art Director: Lawrence Snelly

Layout & Typesetting: Jeff Holt

Interior Art: Guy Davis, Larry MacDougall, Richard Kane Ferguson, Michael Gaydos, Leif Jones, Vince Locke, William O'Connor, Andrew Trabbold

Front Cover Art: Miran Kim

Front & Back Cover Design: Jeff Holt

735 PARK NORTH BLVD.
SUITE 128
CLARKSTON, GA 30021
USA

Check out White Wolf online at

http://www.white-wolf.com; alt.games.whitewolf and rec.games.frp.storyteller

PRINTED IN USA.

TABLE OF CONTENTS

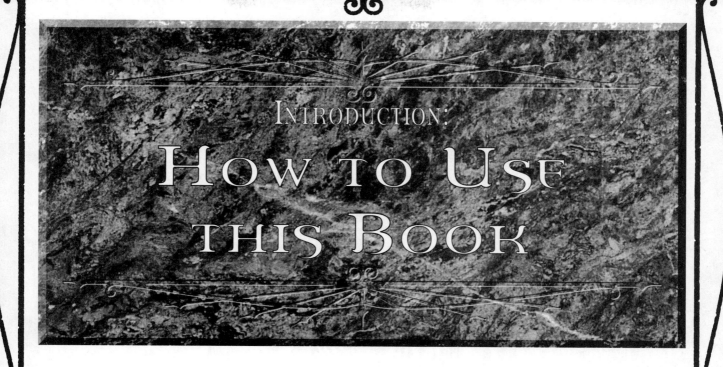

Introduction: How to Use this Book

Welcome. Won't you please come in?

By now, you likely have a sense for the malignancy and mystery of the World of Darkness. Your mind conjures images of soaring gothic cathedrals, looming shadows, skyscrapers arrogantly reaching heavenward and nightclubs teeming with masses of nihilistic humanity.

You also know that among all these lurk the Kindred. Like parasites, the vampires spread themselves insidiously among the people from whom they steal their nightly existence. This book concerns those Kindred, and specifically the stories you and your troupe can tell about them.

To some extent, this book is the "overflow" from the **Vampire: The Masquerade** core rulebook — it helps round out the world but it isn't vital to every story. Some parts of this book, like the bloodlines and Disciplines, are included to allow Storytellers the opportunity to throw new mysteries at their players. Other aspects, like Secondary Abilities and Equipment, give Storytellers new rules and systems to add greater complexity (and a bit of brand-name flash) to their troupe's chronicles.

Remember that mystery when integrating these ideas into your **Vampire** stories — there's no reason characters or players should know any of the details herein unless they are bona-fide scholars in their field. The bloodlines are rare, the new Abilities are very specific, and unless your characters are soldiers or gun-runners, they're unlikely to know a Glock from a Gangrel. Reveal the shadowy movements of the undead to your troupe with the patience of a brooding Methuselah — it will be a better, more intense game for your efforts.

That said, here's what this book examines:

Chapter One: Bloodlines looks at three of the lesser "families" of Kindred. Their origins shrouded in mystery, these vampires prowl the modern nights, hiding from the domineering Camarilla and diabolical Sabbat alike.

Chapter Two: Secondary Abilities provides new and more in-depth Traits for characters to study. These new Abilities are more focused than the basic 30 covered in the main rulebook, but are still distinct enough to warrant a mention. Systems are included to create your own Abilities as well, to reflect the unique nature of the Kindred in your World of Darkness.

Chapter Three: Disciplines discusses the frightening (and sometimes infamous) vampiric powers possessed by the Kindred revealed in Chapter One. These secrets are closely guarded by the vampires who practice them — who knows how they will affect unfamiliar Kindred who observe them?

Chapter Four: Equipment looks at personal accouterments for the World of Darkness. This chapter takes a decidedly martial tone, given the precarious nature of physical conflict. Just remember that turnabout is fair play: Characters who resort to violence too often may encounter better-skilled and equipped opponents to handle the threat they pose.

Finally, there is an expanded **Character Sheet** at the end of the book, for players and Storytellers who prefer a convenient, accessible place to keep their characters' darkest secrets.

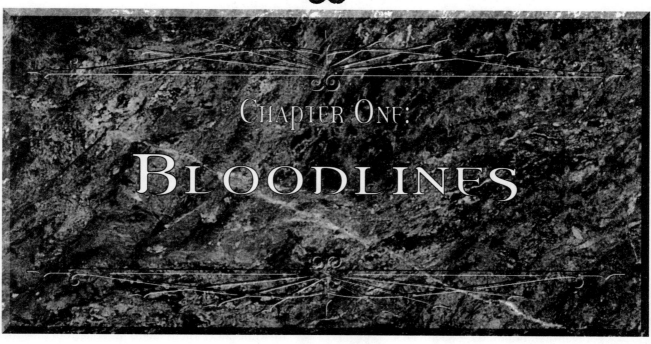

CHAPTER ONE:
BLOODLINES

Kindred blood is a mystical, curious thing. The traits it passes down from sire to childe sometimes remain the same for thousands of years, while at other times it may inexplicably warp or gradually change over time.

The following pages contain bloodlines — families of vampires whose blood has deviated and left them different from their unknown progenitors. Exactly how bloodlines come about is a mystery, but one thing is certain — these vampires are very rare. In the dark world populated by the Kindred, it is uncommon enough to run across a member of one of the more populous clans, let alone one of these. They should appear only sparingly. Also, Storytellers should have no qualms about disallowing these bloodlines from players' options. Use them if you want them, or simply rule that there just aren't any in your chronicle's city.

Daughters of Cacophony

As far as the Kindred are concerned, the Daughters of Cacophony are a modern bloodline, coming into being only within the last few centuries. Many vampires believe this curious bloodline to be the product of mystical unions between Toreador and Malkavians, but little in the bloodline's obscure history indicates that it is anything other than an anomaly, or perhaps the result of a particularly gifted Caitiff.

Whatever their origin, the Daughters of Cacophony are singers extraordinaire, possessed of supernaturally magnificent (or terrifying) voices. Their voices, however, are known for something other than their mystical allure. Through singing, a Daughter of Cacophony may fracture the minds of those who hear her. Darker tales tell of Daughters who can shatter objects — and individuals — with their voices as a mortal singer shatters a glass.

Few Kindred in the Old World have heard much about the Daughters of Cacophony and even fewer have had the opportunity to meet one. The bloodline's presence seems to be largely in the New World, and of little influence.

The Daughters of Cacophony are often considered inconsequential by those Kindred with whom they share domain. Whether it is because the bloodline largely avoids the nightly perils of the Jyhad, or because it is not typically martially or politically inclined, Camarilla and Sabbat alike tend to ignore the Daughters. In their complacency, however, they have ignored much that has occurred in the modern nights of the bloodline. Whereas the bloodline once admitted male members, it has recently culled them from its ranks for reasons unknown. Additionally, a few Kindred have reported that the Daughters' power seems to be increasing — their mysterious songs may be tuned to wreak greater havoc than before, and their blood appears more potent. When confronted with these rumors, the Daughters simply nod and smile, singing as if they hadn't a care.

Naturally, the Daughters are silent as to their greater agenda, if indeed any exists at all. They prefer to while away their nights in song, offering their musical interludes to each other and small, intimate collectives of those who follow their undead careers knowingly or otherwise. They tend to associate with Toreador, Ventrue and Malkavian Kindred, all of whom seem to be able to appreciate the unnatural beauty of their songs, and sometimes become entangled in the machinations of these Kindred.

Daughters of Cacophony, when they can be bothered with issues so peripheral to their interests, sometimes fall in with whichever sect exerts the greatest influence in their immediate surroundings. They seem to abide by the Masquerade, but whether or not they actually care is not obvious — it may be that they see no need to expose themselves for what they are to the mortals around them. More than one account has circulated, however, of Daughters of Cacophony spending nights with elders of both sects and the independents and leaving them maddened after a particularly rousing concert.

Nickname: Sirens

Sect: As a bloodline, the Daughters of Cacophony care little for politics, and have no "official" affiliation with either the Camarilla or the Sabbat. Most Daughters find Sabbat cities brutal and uncomfortable, though, and typically establish residence in Camarilla cities or locales in which they are the only vampires present.

Appearance: The Daughters of Cacophony vary widely in appearance, from rail-thin waifs to rotund opera divas. Members of the bloodline affect clothes and manners that befit their musical niche; the Daughters have their share of leather-clad punk-band frontwomen, satin-dressed piano ingenues and everything in between.

Haven: The Daughters make havens wherever suits their tastes, which may be derelict warehouses, high-rise condominium developments or even the opera houses in which they perform. They typically hide their havens from other Kindred, relying on isolation to protect them.

Background: The bloodline Embraces only those females who possess alluring or noteworthy voices. These individuals need not be singers or musicians in life, though most were. Daughters of Cacophony come from all strata of society, chosen for their singing ability above any other concerns (except gender, of course).

Character Creation: Daughters of Cacophony often have entertainer or performer concepts. Nature and Demeanor may be anything, but most often reflect a predilection for the limelight. Most favor Social Attributes, and cultivate Expression and Performance Abilities. Daughters almost always possess some degree of Fame, and a Herd of admirers commonly surrounds a given Siren.

Clan Disciplines: Fortitude, Melpominee, Presence

Weaknesses: The Daughters of Cacophony, upon their Embrace, become almost trapped by the music that circulates through their souls. Like the Toreador, who become entranced by beauty they observe, the Daughters of Cacophony often lose themselves in the melodic strains that only they can hear. Some Kindred postulate that *all* Daughters hear the same ephemeral tunes, but the Daughters themselves have offered no insight. The difficulties of Perception rolls are increased by one for Daughters of Cacophony, and no Daughter may ever have an Alertness Trait above three, as she is continually distracted by her inner music.

Organization: The Daughters have no formal organization — their numbers are so few and far between that any given location is unlikely to be home for more than one or two of them (if any). When Daughters do congregate for whatever reason, the younger members of the bloodline often defer to the older ones. Some Kindred have been witness to small assemblies of Daughters who perform songs of haunting beauty or frightening timbre that leave their audiences… moved. It has been noted by observant Kindred more than once that even in the most impromptu of performances, all Daughters present seem to know *exactly* what will be sung in addition to all the verses….

Quote: *Why do we sing? Because we must. The noisome undercurrent that passes through each of us must be let to the surface, or it will boil us from within. Let it never be said that an undead heart feels no passion.*

STEREOTYPES

Camarilla: It is an ivory column that does little for us other than provide sometime patrons.

Sabbat: Like an unruly crowd at a concert, the Sabbat sends itself into frenzies at the smell of its own blood.

THE VIEW FROM WITHOUT

The Camarilla

Their songs are at once captivating and deadly — much like I suspect the Sirens to be themselves.

— Jan Pieterzoon, childe of Hardestadt

The Sabbat

Most of them just want to be left alone, and they're not as shady as the other independents. You may as well let them be. Unless you don't want to, of course.

— Dezra, Sabbat flunky

The Independents

Pleasant diversions or manipulable tools — and nothing more.

— Verdigris, Setite mistress

SALUBRI

The Salubri bloodline is surrounded by a miasma of tragedy, loss and hostility. It is rumored that only seven Salubri exist at any given time — after reaching Golconda, a Salubri Embraces a carefully selected childe, who then destroys her sire via diablerie. Few Salubri lead unlives longer than a few hundred years, as they consider the Curse of Caine to be almost unbearable, and most exist for only a few decades before selecting childer and destroying themselves. Exactly how this bloodline attains Golconda so quickly and often is unknown (if indeed they do), and many Kindred suspect deception or outside influence.

Most Kindred perceive the Salubri as diablerists and murderers, largely due to Clan Tremere's ceaseless propaganda campaign against them. The Tremere use their influence to have blood hunts called upon the Salubri at the slightest implication that one may be passing through Camarilla cities. The Salubri's reputation as "soulsuckers" precedes them wherever they go.

According to the tales presented by individual Salubri, they were once a true clan, founded by an enigmatic Kindred known as Saulot, the first vampire to achieve Golconda. This achievement came only after Saulot, who had grown disillusioned with the corruption of the Kindred, went into the lands of the East for an untold period of time. When he returned, he bore a mysterious third eye on his forehead and commanded powers no other Kindred had seen before. He also told of an escape from the hell of vampiric existence — Golconda. After his return, he sired few new childer. Some attribute the creation of the Inconnu and the Brujah's fabled Carthage to Saulot's aid.

Whatever the truth, the Salubri believe Saulot came back changed in more than mind and body. They believe he sired his last childe during Caligula's rule and thereafter grew isolated, tending to his childer's pursuit of Golconda. This isolation proved his undoing, however. At some unknown point in time, he entered torpor, perhaps voluntarily. During the Middle Ages, a group of power-hungry magi unearthed Saulot's resting place. The most powerful of these magi slew the Ancient, slaking his own thirst on Saulot's blood. It is said that Saulot did not resist, knowing that it was his time to pass. To complete the deed, the cabal of magi hunted Saulot's childer to near extinction.

The modern Salubri are the lineage of those of Saulot's brood who managed to escape the purge led by the magi, at least according to what information they told others. The magi are believed to hunt them to this very night, and likely have some connection to the Tremere.

While the Salubri maintain that they are healers, other Kindred believe them to be despoilers and thieves of souls. They are persecuted and hunted, unable to use their healing powers without revealing who they are. Few Kindred would risk "healing" at the hands of the Salubri anyway, fearing that their souls — already in jeopardy due to the Curse of Caine — would be stolen in the process.

The greatest threat to an individual Salubri is, however ironically, herself, as all Salubri sacrifice themselves when they sire new childer by forcing those childer to diablerize them. The Salubri believe that all souls are damned, and only by attaining Golconda can one transcend the torment that awaits them after death. Kindred — and kine — who fail to reach Golconda become ghosts trapped in between the worlds of the living and the dead. Of course, being Kindred is no easy task, and it is a trial that tests the strength of an individual's soul. As such, Salubri are dedicated proselytizers, and their "propaganda" is probably the source of much the antipathy other Kindred feel toward them. Thus, the Salubri eke out secret, desperate unlives, hounded by their fellow Kindred who refuse to see the truths put before them.

Nickname: Soulsuckers or Cyclops

Sect: The Salubri are shunned (at best) and actively hunted (at worst) by both Camarilla and Sabbat. Neither sect will have them, not that the Salubri would join either anyway.

Appearance: There is no uniform look among the Salubri — they are so few and choose progeny on such individual basis that no generalization exists. Children, elderly, the middle-aged and young adults have all populated the ranks of the Salubri at one time or another, and have hailed from all walks of life.

The Salubri do bear one physical trait in common, however. All Salubri develop a third eye in the middle of their foreheads around the time they learn the second level of Obeah. This third eye, which is the same color as their normal eyes, opens any time an Obeah power of second level or greater is in use. When the eye is closed, it is barely noticeable; the eyeslit appears as nothing more than a subtle scar. The purpose of this eye and its origins are unknown, but most Kindred who have any familiarity at all with the Salubri posit that it grants the Cyclops "sight beyond sight" or infernal visions. Salubri Kindred often hide their third eyes by wearing Gypsy-style headscarves or hats with shading brims, or behind long bangs.

Haven: When Salubri are able to establish permanent havens, they typically do so far from the domains of other Kindred. Salubri make their havens in desolate places, away from the vindictive eyes of others, and typically keep few physical possessions (the better to travel quickly).

Background: The Salubri prefer to Embrace individuals with high Humanity: healers, holy folk, philanthropists, environmentalists and the like. Supposedly, only seven Salubri exist at any one time, though some Kindred report that this number may be less in the modern nights — or more….

Character Creation: Salubri may have any concept, though it is unlikely that they will be criminals or soldiers. Natures and Demeanors tend toward the altruistic, though the latter may be literally anything. Most Salubri favor Mental Attributes and Knowledges, though there have been exceptions in the past. All Salubri must take five dots worth of Generation to represent their sires' sacrifice; many Salubri also have a few points in the Herd Background.

Clan Disciplines: Auspex, Fortitude, Obeah

Weaknesses: Salubri may take blood only from those who give it willingly. If a Salubri's vessel resists her attempt to feed, the Salubri loses a point from her Willpower pool and may have to check for Humanity degeneration at the Storyteller's discretion.

Organization: The Salubri are too few to have an actual "organization," though most of the bloodline follow a similar code. To the Salubri, the pursuit of Golconda is paramount, and they seem loath to refuse aid to each other. The Salubri are a loyal lot, and what they lack in organization they make up for with dedication. Only the most desperate Salubri would compromise another's safety — most would choose death before dishonor. Some elder Kindred claim to have observed a more cavalier attitude in the modern Salubri, however, and perhaps a bit of overt cruelty. Salubri communicate through cryptic words scribed in a forgotten language. In nights past, the Salubri would carve these messages on trees or other markers they would pass for other Salubri to see. In the modern nights, they may "tag" an area in the manner of graffiti or simply write a message and leave it for someone to deliver to a clanmate obliviously.

All recognized Salubri are of the Eighth Generation (conferred by the sires' sacrifice at a new childe's Embrace). Persistent rumors continue to surface, however, of powerful Kindred traveling from the East bearing the third eye of Saulot.

Quote: *Your soul is sick, stained by the Curse of Caine. Offer it up to me and I shall cleanse it. You must trust me, for an eternity of damnation is more than you could bear. I know.*

STEREOTYPES

Camarilla: They are so obsessed with hiding their evil they cannot feel the Tremere's fangs at their throats. The Camarilla is too blind and selfish to learn from our example.

Sabbat: Damnation is not the gore-splattered romp they believe it to be. They gladly desecrate their souls without a second thought.

THE VIEW FROM WITHOUT

The Camarilla

Those who truck with the Salubri risk their souls, not merely their blood.

— Rex Foster, Tremere apprentice

The Sabbat

Whipped dogs. Kick them like the puling wretches they are.

— Vincent Day, Sabbat paladin

The Independents

They make a huge issue of some long-forgotten ill they received. Cry me a river.

— Anja Kazmierz, Ravnos nomad

SAMEDI

The Samedi are vampires of especially unwholesome ilk, and dreadful to look upon. Their bodies resemble corpses, and those who see them sometimes mistake them for zombies or other revenant horrors.

Thought to have originated in the Caribbean, the Samedi have strong ties to the region's voodoo legacies. They practice a unique Discipline that allows them to manipulate the energies of death, albeit in a much more temporal manner than Giovanni Necromancy. Indeed, the Giovanni have very little good to say about the Samedi, and the enmity between these Kindred runs deep. Some Kindred believe that the Samedi are the result of a vile Giovanni experiment gone wrong, while other vampires attribute darker origins to the Stiffs. Still other Kindred believe that the Samedi are a derelict offshoot of the Nosferatu — one that should have been stillborn.

Samedi often involve themselves with occult or illegal activities in a city, becoming powerful *houngans* and *mambos* or trafficking with superstitious immigrant criminal elements. Given their apparent voodoo roots, the Samedi seem content to garner influence in immigrant ghettoes, practicing their dark magic and preying upon a populace used to the dead walking among them.

The Samedi are also notorious assassins and mercenaries, and it is for this reason that many Camarilla princes turn a blind eye to them in spite of their almost Masquerade-threatening involvement with the kine around them. For the most part, the Samedi keep to themselves, and a prince never knows when she may need an ally with "special" abilities. The Stiffs seem to hold the Nosferatu and Giovanni in some inscrutable esteem (or dread), though, as they are hesitant to take out contracts on Kindred of these clans without just cause or considerable payment.

There is more to the Samedi bloodline than a loose association of witch-doctors and death cultists, however. The bloodline is insular and secretive; many times, its members often keep their affairs private from even other members, suggesting that they have something other than common interests. A few Samedi are known to be members of the Camarilla or Sabbat, but these offer those sects little information on others of their kind. Arguably the eldest member of the bloodline, a vampire known only as the Baron, suggests that the Samedi have a greater role in the Kindred's history and future than most vampires suspect. What that may be, the Baron refuses to specify, dismissing further questions with a wave of his rotting hand.

Nickname: Stiffs

Sect: The Samedi claim membership in no sect, though individual Stiffs may be found in the Camarilla and Sabbat when they choose to bother with such things.

Appearance: Samedi Kindred look like corpses in various — usually advanced — stages of decomposition. Some Samedi are putrid, with foul fluids oozing from their tattered skin, while others are leathery, emaciated and look like unwrapped mummies. The eyes of Samedi vampires sink deep into their skulls upon the Embrace and their lips retract, exposing a horrid rictus of teeth and fangs. Additionally, most Samedi lose their noses once Embraced as well, leaving gaping pits in the center of their faces (though this does not seem to affect their ability to smell scents).

Haven: Samedi make their havens in areas associated with death, so that they attract no more undue attention than is possible. The Stiffs prefer mausoleums, crypts, graveyards, funeral homes and even ill-attended morgues. A few Samedi have taken to dwelling with Nosferatu in tunnels beneath their cities, but the Nosferatu tend to find the Samedi too morbid for much long-term cohabitation.

Background: The Samedi seem to be a modern phenomenon, and no Samedi is suspected to be more than 250 years old, even after their Embrace. In light of this, however, the Samedi seem more numerous than they have in the past few decades, particularly in the voodoo-influenced regions of the Caribbean and the southern United States. These Kindred are typically loners, and it is uncommon to find more than two making permanent havens in any given city, no matter the size. Many Samedi claim to have worked in fields related to death during their mortal lives — coroners, morticians, witch doctors, etc. — and almost as many admit to being suicidal at one point or another before their Embrace.

Character Creation: Samedi typically Embrace those with a penchant for death, a trait that follows them into undeath. Many Samedi favor Mental Attributes and Knowledges while the martial, mercenary members of the bloodline cultivate Physical Attributes and Skills or Talents. Samedi rarely have Herd, Mentor or Resources Backgrounds. A significant percentage of the Samedi bloodline, particularly the older members, practices the Discipline of Necromancy but it is unknown precisely where they would have come across this knowledge, as they appear to be on very poor terms with the Giovanni.

Clan Disciplines: Fortitude, Obfuscate, Thanatosis

Weaknesses: Samedi are hideous to behold, albeit in a different manner than the Nosferatu. Whereas the Nosferatu are disfigured and monstrous, the Samedi are much more corpselike and decayed. The fetid stench of the grave follows the Stiffs as well, and their decomposed skin is nauseating to the touch. All Samedi suffer Appearance Traits of 0, which may never be increased (though it may be hidden or changed mystically).

Organization: The Samedi are so few that if an organization or hierarchy exists, no one understands it except the bloodline itself. On the rare nights when two Samedi come in contact with each other, they may pause only briefly to exchange news or rumors before parting ways. A few turbulent rumors sweep through Kindred society about secret cabals of Samedi gathering in graveyards, but none of these rumors have been substantiated.

Quote: *Do I frighten you? Do I disgust you? A thousand pardons! Here, let me help you — let me show you what it is like to bear this curse. Come, feel the cold, foul kiss of true undeath.*

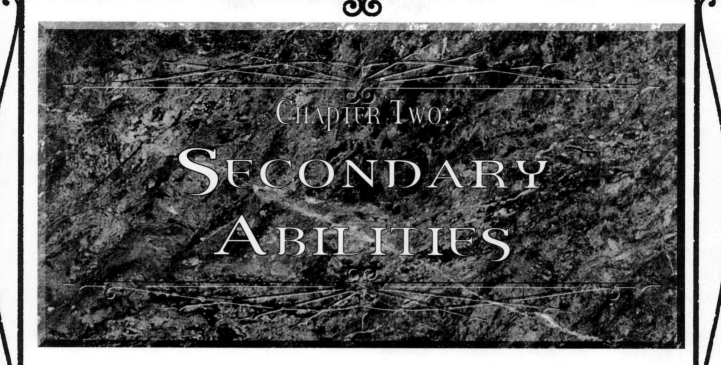

CHAPTER TWO:
SECONDARY ABILITIES

The following Abilities are for use in **Vampire: The Masquerade**. They are more specialized than the primary ones, but are generally distinct enough to be Abilities in their own right rather than specialties of the primary ones.

One Ability point buys two dots in Secondary Abilities during character creation (though they may not be purchased above three without freebie points, like Primary Abilities), and one freebie point buys one dot. Raising a Secondary Ability with experience points costs the current rating in experience points — a number of points equal to the level the player desires (though Abilities may not be increased by more than one in between any given stories). Additionally, some Secondary Abilities here (Masquerade, Camarilla and Sabbat Lore, and City Secrets) should not be available to new vampires, and others (Demolitions) are remarkably hard to find training in.

There are still some tasks that your troupe may decide don't really fall under any existing Ability. For these, the Hobby Talent, Professional Skill and Expert Knowledge Abilities have been provided. These may be made into virtually anything that you think your character should have a rating in. However, this is always subject to Storyteller approval. Some things may fit better as specialties of existing Abilities. Professional Skill: Lockpicking, for instance, would fit under Security. Some other Traits may not be what the Storyteller really wants in her game, such as Expert Knowledge: Nuclear Warhead Engineering. As always, the Storyteller is the final authority in such matters.

As a final note, use of these Secondary Abilities is purely optional — Storytellers should feel free not to use these or to permit only certain ones. Secondary Abilities add greater complexity to a game, but they also add greater complication. If your game is fine without them, forget about them.

TALENTS
GRACE

Veronica sauntered into the Digital Lounge without bothering to pay the cover — they knew her here. She caught Andrei's eye and made her way to the table where one of the city's prominent anarchs conducted business.

"What the hell do you want?" Andrei snarled before she could open her mouth to explain. "I thought I told you to stay out of here!" He motioned for two of his ghouls to remove her.

Veronica spitted the nearer of the two with a glare that could have curdled milk, then turned a dazzling smile on Andrei. "I'm here to apologize for my previous behavior, in a way. Let me get you a drink...."

Andrei snorted, "Buy me a drink in my own bar? You've been feeding from too many crackheads."

"Actually, I brought something a little more to your... personal taste." Veronica beckoned, and the twin blood dolls she'd found earlier that night stepped forward. Andrei stared, entranced, and Veronica's earlier transgressions vanished in a haze of lust and hunger.

This is the ability to function "smoothly" in a social setting. Gossiping, cutting deals in the halls of power, making a good first impression on a visiting archon and handling yourself in an elder salon are all aspects of Grace. Graceless characters may be boorish, introverted or under-socialized; conversely, characters with high Grace ratings get along with people in any crowd and often have high Contacts ratings.

- •   Novice: Debutante
- ••   Practiced: Senator
- •••   Competent: Hollywood celebrity
- ••••   Expert: Public relations director
- ••••• Master: Vampire prince

Possessed by: Elder Kindred, Politicians, Socialites, Media Personalities, Toreador

Specialties: First Impressions, Gossip, Rumor Control, Schemes, Veiled Threats and Innuendoes

INSTRUCTION

Johanna surveyed her basement with a scowl of disgust. "Pathetic," she muttered. "Absolutely pathetic. We're at war, and you can't even manage a basic exercise!"

One of the zhupan's ghouls reached tentatively through the door, tugging at Johanna's sleeve. He cringed as she turned on him angrily, "Yes, yes, I know the others are waiting! I'll be but a moment!" She turned back to her class. "Now, try it again. First the teeth, then retract the bone, then smooth the flesh over." She paused and sneered, "You may feed... once you restore your faces."

Behind Johanna, her five new childer burbled and clawed at the air with misshapen appendages.

"Those who can, do; those who can't, teach," goes the saying. Actually, those who can make the best teachers, but they still need this Ability to pass their expertise on to others. Any Skill or Knowledge can be taught to another character. Talents can be developed on one's own, though some (such as Brawl) may be taught, and Disciplines may be taught with the Storyteller's approval. The teacher cannot pass on a higher level of the subject than her level of Instruction. For instance, if Johanna has Occult 5 but only Instruction 3, she cannot teach her childer a higher level of Occult than 3. She has the information herself, but she doesn't have the means to convey such advanced information to her pupils.

Every month spent Instructing a pupil allows the instructor to make a Manipulation + Instruction roll (difficulty of 10 - the student's Intelligence, or 9 - Intelligence if the student has the Merit *Quick Learner*). Each success on this roll gives the student one experience point to put toward the Skill, Knowledge or Discipline in question. Studies require a substantial amount of downtime, and students may be required to make Intelligence, Wits or Willpower rolls to embrace particularly difficult (quantum physics) or traumatizing (fire-walking) subjects.

- • Novice: Boy Scout merit badge instructor
- •• Practiced: Elementary school teacher
- ••• Competent: Calculus IV professor
- •••• Expert: World-renowned lecturer in your chosen field
- ••••• Master: Socrates

Possessed by: Teachers, Drill Instructors, Wise Ones, People Everywhere

Specialties: Dialectics, Lore, Gifted Students, Lecture

INTERROGATION

Kleist tapped his fingers on the table. Across from him, a battered vampire wrapped in steel tow cables glared sullenly at him, mostly unrumpled from the night's exertions. Kleist spoke in crisp tones, "I have other appointments tonight, whelp. You can tell me where the rest of your pack is, or I can resort to drastic measures."

The prisoner spat a glob of half-congealed blood onto the floor. Kleist sighed and turned to his assistant. "Jaeger, would you bring me my tools?"

"Of course, sir. Will you be using the rib spreader tonight?" Kleist pursed his lips thoughtfully, studying the ragged Sabbat. "No, bring me a pair of scissors, a jar of sand and the blowtorch."

The prisoner's eyes widened. "Oh, God, no! Wait — please! Commerce — they're at 32 Commerce Street! In the lofts!"

"Why, thank you. You certainly have an active imagination," Kleist chuckled.

The fine art of making people talk takes many forms. Interrogation can be as subtle as a well-intentioned psychoanalysis or as crude as a handful of rusty nails and a hammer. Many skilled interrogators don't think of themselves as such, and some have never had any formal training whatsoever. The masters of this field have reputations that are sometimes as effective as the interrogations themselves.

- • Novice: Small-town newspaper reporter
- •• Practiced: Vice cop
- ••• Competent: Psychiatrist
- •••• Expert: KGB "physician"
- ••••• Master: *Voivode* from the Old World

Possessed by: Cops, Inquisitors, Psychiatrists, Tzimisce, War Criminals

Specialties: Agony, Casual Conversation, Good Cop/Bad Cop, Journalism, Long-Term Brainwashing, Threats Against Family Members

INTUITION

"Are you sure no one's going to find us?" whined Michael. Ben glared at him. "Of course not! The Camarilla's too disorganized here, too caught up in its own infight—"

A spotlight snapped on, pinning the two scouts in its harsh glare. From the shadows of the warehouse stepped a dozen or more figures, guns and claws glimmering. A misshapen silhouette in a rumpled suit strode into the light. "Indeed. Too disorganized. Too complacent. Too incompetent to notice a Sabbat incursion." His

speech dripped with sarcasm. "Some, maybe, but we watch. We always watch."

Ben found his voice. "How'd you know we were here?"

A chuckle. "Call it a hunch. You were good — very good — at covering your tracks, but you left bits and pieces. Not enough for analysis, but enough for a guess." The archon turned away. "Take them."

Unquantifiable and indefinable, Intuition is the quality that lets some individuals sort clues from a sea of false information and *feel* with perfect clarity when something is right. It covers a wide array of minor yet critical tasks, from sensing when a ghoul's lying to you to realizing that your opponent is bluffing his way through his hand to putting clues together when the sum of the parts doesn't quite equal the whole. Intuition is sixth sense, gut feelings and hunches. It is an excellent Talent for the Storyteller to drop clues through if the players are going astray.

- • Novice: Your guesses usually point you in the right direction.
- •• Practiced: Your first answer is usually the best.
- ••• Competent: You get a funny feeling when your suspicions are valid.
- •••• Expert: You sense what's wrong and who's behind it.
- ••••• Master: Your insights come with perfect clarity.

Possessed by: Gamblers, Zen Masters, Investigators, Fortune Tellers, Bodyguards

Specialties: Sense Lies, Gambling, Trouble, Flashes of Inspiration

MASQUERADE

The paramedic frowned. "You really should have some X-rays taken. Your pulse is very weak, and I can't tell for certain if those ribs are broken or just bruised."

Ramona shrugged, obviously trying not to wince. "I'm okay, really. They don't feel bad enough to be broken, and my pulse is always weak — low blood pressure, y'know."

"All right. Not too much more I can do for you here. If you start feeling any more pain, have someone drive you to the hospital immediately, all right?" The paramedic wiped tiredly at his face and turned back to the devastated nightclub.

Ramona slipped away into the crowd of onlookers, easily avoiding the knot of television cameras taking in the scene. Quickly finding a pay phone, she slipped a pair of quarters into it and dialed. "Blake? It's me. I had to play hurt to be able to listen in on the cops without being interrogated as a witness, but I think I know who started the riot...."

This Talent cannot be taken by starting characters, and is (obviously) available only to vampires. It is the ability to falsely reproduce the frailties and subtle clues of mortality: respiration, creating a pulse, forcing blood to the skin to appear flushed, sneezing, slowing reflexes to mortal speed, et al. Masquerade may be rolled with a Social Attribute to

determine how well the vampire fools the mortals around him — any vampire can pretend to breathe, but not every vampire can do it *well*.

- • Novice: You can pass in an unobservant crowd.
- •• Practiced: You can fool a casual observer.
- ••• Competent: You can fool someone who's examining you.
- •••• Expert: You can pass a routine physical exam.
- ••••• Master: Even the Society of Leopold would think you mortal.

Possessed by: Vampires

Specialties: Breathing, Heartbeat, Skin Tone and Warmth, Sleep, Reflexes and Muscle Twitches, Sexuality

MIMICRY

Blake nodded into the phone. "Well done, Ramona. Hang around there for a while longer and see what else you can learn. I'll send someone to pick you up in a bit." He hung up and coughed twice, then picked up the handset and dialed again.

"It's Blake," he said, his voice dropping an octave and his accent changing from light Creole to Deep South. "She bought it. Thinks she's still dealing with Xaviar's people. She'll be waiting around the riot scene for someone to come pick her up. Send someone to get her."

Whether the desired sound is a Romanian accent, a bird call or the bark of an attack dog, a talented mimic can reproduce it. With enough practice, the amazingly flexible human (or vampiric) larynx can be used to create almost any sort of sound. Most mechanical noises, however, are best left to sound technicians with the proper synthesizers — whistling to the fax machine is right out.

- • Novice: You can fake accents in your native language (Texas or New York for an American, for instance), and can probably do impressions of the voices of a few well-known personalities.
- •• Practiced: You can manage accents well enough to fool anyone but a native speaker (a German speaker impersonating Japanese-accented German), and can convincingly duplicate a wide range of celebrities.
- ••• Competent: You could make a living with a stage act. After studying a subject for a few hours, you can pick up their speech patterns and mannerisms well enough to fool anyone who doesn't know them. You can also manage birdcalls and some other natural sounds.
- •••• Expert: You can imitate a specific person well enough to fool even a close acquaintance, as long as she can't see you. With command of the appropriate language, you can pass as a native speaker, even faking various regional and dialectal accents.
- ••••• Master: There is almost no accent or animal you can't imitate. With a few hours' study, either of the real person or of recordings, you can duplicate their voice and speech patterns well enough to fool their closest friends.

Possessed By: Actors, Linguists, Sound Technicians, Pranksters, Birdwatchers

Specialties: Accents, Celebrities, Birds and Animals, Studied Subjects

STYLE

Every conversation in the room stopped suddenly as Maris entered the ballroom, and all eyes fell on her. She was a picturesque beauty, the silk of her dress cascading off her lithe form like a waterfall. Maris wore her dark hair pinned high atop her head, accentuating her sharp cheekbones and contrasting the deep burgundy of her lips. A simple black wrap enveloped her like the gossamer clouds that surround angels. This was no angel, however; no, this was something far less wholesome....

Style is the fine art of knowing how to dress appropriately — which isn't necessarily the same as knowing how to dress *well*. You may not be the best-looking or most charming of the bunch, but you know how to use what you have. Heads turn when you walk into a room, simply because you can make yourself match any occasion or location, from a black-tie Toreador art show to a warehouse rave. Characters with high Style ratings may have large wardrobes or may simply wear one thing well (like Johnny Cash). Style encompasses clothing choice, poise and even coordinating or designing new outfits. A minimum of Style 3 is necessary to incorporate body armor into street clothing without it being obvious (see the Equipment chapter).

Note that Style differs from Grace in that Style is *looking* cool, while Grace is *acting* cool.

- • Novice: You've got good taste.
- •• Practiced: Your friends always take you along for advice when they go shopping.
- ••• Competent: You stand out among the sheep.
- •••• Expert: Your outfits grace the bodies of magazine fashion models.
- ••••• Master: Your ideas influence international fashion trends.

Possessed By: Socialites, Models, Designers, Theatrical Wardrobe Staff, the Gifted Few

Specialties: Classic, Ethnic, Street Fashion, Haute Couture, First Impressions

THROWING

Thunk.

Dutch turned away from the dartboard. "I think that's game, boys. Now if you'd be so kind...?"

"What the hell are you doing?" Corey asked impatiently.

"Just making a little bit of spending money, as it were. A little friendly competition, that's all." Dutch's hand strayed inside his sleeve for a moment. "And keeping in practice in case things don't stay friendly."

Making things fly that aren't really designed to is not an easy task. Throwing encompasses both casual (e.g. sporting) and combat uses of this Talent.

- •   Novice: You can usually get a pitch over the plate.
- ••   Practiced: You were feared in food fights.
- •••   Competent: Your squadmates never had to duck when you were on the grenade practice range.
- •••• Expert: You can pin an enemy's hand to the wall or make a 70-yard touchdown pass.
- ••••• Master: You can pin an enemy's pants to the wall without touching his skin.

Possessed By: Athletes, Hobbyists, Neighborhood Pub Locals, Martial Artists

Specialties: Sports, Specific Projectiles, Trick Shots, Competition

VENTRILOQUISM

"Over here, big guy!"

"No, over here!"

"Whoops, now I'm over here!"

The hunter cursed and spun, leveling his shotgun at every dancing shadow large enough to harbor his prey. "Hell-spawned bitch, your demon ways won't save you from the wrath of our Lord!"

"No, actually, my drama-school tricks will save me to-night." Her voice came from behind him, and the hunter had just enough time to first disregard it, then realize he should have paid more attention….

You have the ability to throw your voice, making it sound as if it's coming from somewhere — or someone — else. This Talent can be used for either entertainment or deception, and can be combined with Mimicry for even more effect in either application. Note that Ventriloquism and Mimicry, while compatible, cannot be substituted for one another — they are completely different areas of vocal manipulation.

- •   Novice: You and your dummy can do children's birthday parties.
- ••   Practiced: You could get an act with a local vaudeville club. Someone standing next to you can be made to "speak."
- •••   Competent: You could almost make a living on small comedy club tours. Your maximum range for throwing your voice is five yards.
- •••• Expert: Vegas would welcome your talent. Any spot within 30 feet of you can be used as your target.
- ••••• Master: You can project your voice anywhere within earshot. Young hopefuls clamor to learn your tricks, and entertainment magazines hail you as the savior of a lost vaudeville art.

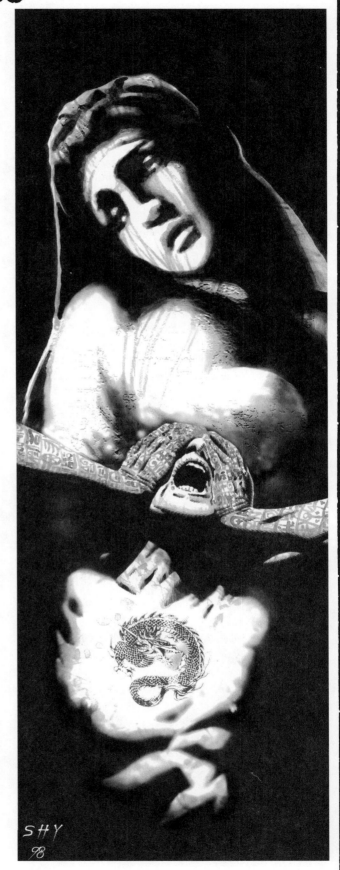

Possessed By: Entertainers, Con Artists, Pranksters, some Mediums

Specialties: Distance, Dummy, Other People, Inanimate Objects

HOBBY TALENT

This category encompasses anything that the Storyteller deems to be mainly self-taught and is usually (though not always — e.g. Style) more active than intellectual. Storytellers should first examine the list of existing Talents and Secondary Talents to determine if a particular activity might fall under one of those (for example, Swimming and Climbing would be specialties of Athletics).

- • Novice: You've dabbled.
- •• Practiced: You've got a good grasp of your hobby's basics.
- ••• Competent: Other practitioners regard you as fairly skilled and competent.
- •••• Expert: You are familiar with the subtle nuances and applications of your Talent.
- ••••• Master: You could write a book on what you do. Perhaps you already have....

Suggested Hobby Talents: Carousing, Diplomacy, Fortune Telling, Negotiation, Scrounging

SKILLS

ARCHERY

"Take this!"

Toshiro glanced at the proffered rifle in his partner's hand. "Thank you, no. Guns have no soul."

"Yeah, and neither will you if that bastard drinks it!"

The door shattered, shards of steel flying as the frenzied vampire burst into the room. Four guns opened up, bullets punching wildly through the walls or flattening against skin six centuries old. The monster roared challenge, lashing out to dismember and rend.

Toshiro drew, focused... waited for the moment of perfect clarity... felt bow and arrow and archer and target become one... and released. The elder's wordless scream cut off abruptly as he crumpled to the floor, his heart transfixed by an oaken shaft.

The archer lowered his bow and smiled faintly. "For some things, the old ways are still the best."

Although bows have long since been supplanted by firearms in the modern world, there are still enough hobbyists and hunters to keep them around. Many Kindred elders, too, remember the nights before gunpowder and still stay in practice. Archery encompasses the use of both regular bows and crossbows as well as their construction and the creation of new arrows (see Archery in the Equipment chapter for minimum Archery values for the construction of various types of bows).

- • Novice: You remember hunting as a mortal archer.
- •• Practiced: If you were still inclined toward eating venison, you could get your own with ease.
- ••• Competent: You may have been a medieval woodsman.
- •••• Expert: Your prowess is nigh legendary.
- ••••• Master: Robin Hood or William Tell

Possessed By: Elder Kindred, Hunters, Hobby Enthusiasts, Competitors, Traditionalists

Specialties: Indirect Fire, Forests, Competition, Precision Shots, Hunting

DEMOLITIONS

"Two minutes. C'mon, Theo, c'mon!"

The Brujah frowned. A single drop of blood-sweat coursed down his forehead. "Easy, kid. It's been 30-some years since I did this." He glanced up absently. "Needle-nose pliers. Is the building clear?"

"Everyone except the prince. He's refusing to leave. Says he's lived here for two centuries."

"Stubborn sonofabitch. Gimme that plastic probe — I need something nonconductive."

"Fifteen seconds. Jesus...."

"Yeah, I know. Right. Cross your fingers. This might hurt...."

Demolitions encompasses both the use of explosives and the knowledge of how to keep them from blowing up at inconvenient times. Characters with this Skill know the proper methods for storing, transporting and using various explosive and incendiary compounds (actually *making* explosives falls under the Chemistry specialty of Science). Proper Demolitions training is extremely hard to come by, and Storytellers should feel no qualms whatsoever about denying characters any rating over 1 in this Skill. Low levels in this Skill are generally the most dangerous, as actual learning experiences involve live explosives and failing a lesson can be fatal. See the Explosives section of the Equipment chapter for more information.

- • Novice: You've read *The Anarchist's Cookbook* and maybe a couple of military handbooks. You can manage pipe bombs or small black powder charges. You are as much of a danger to yourself as to anyone else.
- •• Practiced: You have gone through some basic military training — more of what to *not* do than what to do. You can place premade charges (e.g. satchel charges) if told what to do by a more experienced combat engineer or ordnance technician.
- ••• Competent: You may have been a combat engineer or an ordnance technician. Defusing simple devices is within your capability. You know enough to figure the best way to set a simple shaped charge against an ordinary target. This is the minimum rating necessary to set your own charges from raw materials.

- •••• Expert: If you sought gainful employment, you could easily be hired as an EOD (Explosive Ordnance Disposal) technician, or perhaps made the head of a bomb squad. You can figure out complex, booby-trapped triggering mechanisms, and you know how to position charges to bring down an entire structure.
- ••••• Master: Law enforcement agencies across the globe call you to consult in crises — or to help figure out what happened in the wake of a blast.

Possessed By: Terrorists, Police Bomb Squads, Combat Engineers, Miners, Special Forces Personnel, Militia Members and Wannabes

Specialties: Disarming, Booby Traps, Imploding Buildings, Bomb Detection, Vehicles, Blast Analysis

DISGUISE

Ron frowned and reached for another brush. "Hold still, I said. If you keep moving, the latex won't set right. How do you expect me to do my job like this?"

The Nosferatu squirmed uncomfortably. "Those lights are so hot. Is this really worth it?"

"Well, I need them to dry this. If you want to make a public appearance, you can't rely on your powers to hide you from cameras. Now, which dress are you going to wear? I'll find some colored contacts to match."

Disguise allows you to alter your own appearance and those of others with the proper application of makeup, clothing and props, and, at higher levels, prosthetics. All of these tasks are extremely difficult without access to the proper materials.

- • Novice: You've taken a basic class in stage makeup. You can do some very basic and subtle effects, but impersonating someone else is beyond you.
- •• Practiced: You can fool someone who knows neither you nor the person you're impersonating. You could put together horror-type makeup for a haunted house.
- ••• Competent: You can effect substantial changes in your appearance and Appearance. You can pass casual glances from casual acquaintances.
- •••• Expert: You could find employment as a cinematic makeup technician, and can create a hundred different faces for yourself or your subjects. Gender-switching is not out of the question if your subject can do the voice and body language.
- ••••• Master: A Nosferatu-to-Toreador makeover artist, you can accomplish transformations that most people would think impossible.

Possessed By: Entertainers, Spies, Con Artists, F/X Technicians

Specialties: Theater and Television, False Wounds and Disfigurements, Concealing Identity, Impersonating Others

HERBALISM

"Yes, yes, I know what it does to mortals, but will it work on the prince?"

The Assamite nodded. "We have our ways, Warlock. The formula you provided me has been... refined, and it will be delivered when I am certain I can strike. I trust you have arranged payment?"

"Indeed. Now go, before I'm seen with you. And be quick about your task! I have a personal interest in observing the effects of my—ah, of our work."

The Assassin rose and strode wordlessly down the street. A slight smirk flickered across her otherwise impassive features. "I never said where I'd strike," she murmured once out of earshot. "The prince has an equal interest, it seems, in watching the effects of the ancient formulas upon his less trusted advisors...."

You have a knowledge of herbs and other natural substances and their properties for both medicinal and other applications. You know where such ingredients are likely to be found, and you can gather and preserve them.

- • Novice: You read a book on herb lore once.
- •• Practiced: You learned everything your grandmother had to teach you.
- ••• Competent: You are well-versed in the uses of even rare plants.
- •••• Expert: You are well known in regional and nature-lover circles as a source of wisdom.
- ••••• Master: In the nights of old, you could have been a wealthy apothecary.

Possessed By: Wiccans and Wannabes, Holistic Healers, Alchemists, Medicine Men

Specialties: Cooking, Medicine, Toxins, Narcotics and Hallucinogens, Charms

LIP READING

Hesha strained at his field glasses. "I can't quite make out what he's saying... damn Nosferatu, they don't have any lips to watch. He's... yes... 'My contingent and I will be preparing to depart tonight,' he just told the prince. 'Our presence in your city is no longer necessary.' Good. With that archon out of the way, we'll be able to go ahead. 'We'll be moving on to New York,' I think he said. Are you writing this down?"

You are able to understand speech without hearing the actual words, as long as you can see the subject's mouth moving. Although you can rarely get the entire sentence, you can usually figure out what's being said from context.

- • Novice: If someone talks slowly and enunciates with exaggerated movements, you can get most of it.
- •• Practiced: You can understand if someone talks fairly slowly and you concentrate.
- ••• Competent: You can usually comprehend normal conversation.
- •••• Expert: Even under poor lighting and distance, you can usually make out most of a sentence.
- ••••• Master: Smoke, night and ventriloquism are no barriers to you. You can even make out foreign languages if you speak them fluently.

Possessed By: Spies, Detectives, Hearing-Impaired Individuals

Specialties: Accents, Poor Lighting, Drunks, Fast Talkers, Covert Observation

MEDITATION

"Hey, Hiro, you in here?" The door swung open. "Oh."

One tufted ear swiveled slightly at the intrusion, and a taloned finger twitched minutely on the hilt of the katana. The figure kneeling in the center of the circle of candles made no other acknowledgment, but continued his low, repetitive chant. A slight breeze ruffled the small slips of paper spread on the floor as the door swung shut again.

The moonlit shadows of the trees outside slowly crept across the polished floor. As the first hint of dawn brightened the eastern sky, Hiro fell silent and rose smoothly to his feet. He opened the door and bowed to the anxious faces of his companions. "I believe I have the answer we seek," he intoned quietly.

You are able to enter a state of trance and relaxation in order to focus your mind inward. This can be used to deal with mental and physical problems, to find calm again, or to put together pieces of a puzzle that your conscious mind refuses to grasp. A successful Intelligence + Meditation roll (difficulty 7) is necessary to enter this trance state. Once in trance, each hour can be used to attempt one of the following tasks:

• To regain Willpower, roll Intelligence + Meditation (difficulty 9); each success restores one temporary Willpower point.

• If attempting to solve a riddle or to unite disparate clues, roll Perception + Meditation (difficulty 9); each success lowers the difficulty of your next Investigation or Enigmas roll by one.

• To overcome wound penalties, roll Stamina + Meditation (difficulty of the number of health levels of damage your character has suffered + 2); the number of successes you score is the maximum amount of wound penalty dice you may ignore for the rest of the night. For example, if Hiro's player scores three successes, all dice pool penalties due to injuries are reduced by three, so any penalty up to -3 would be ignored entirely, and a four-die wound penalty would be treated as a one-die penalty. Incapacitated characters are still incapable

of action, regardless of how many wound penalty dice they would be able to ignore for lesser levels of injury. This roll can be made only once per night.

• To steel your character against his Beast, roll Wits + Meditation (difficulty of 10 - Self-Control rating); each success is an extra die you may use in your next roll for your character to resist frenzy. This roll can be made only once per night, and all benefits are lost when your character sleeps at the end of the night.

If the trance is interrupted enough to break it before the hour is up (brief conversation will not interfere but any physical interference will break the trance), all benefits are lost. Meditation also requires a focus — yogic positions, chanting, etc. — to be effective, otherwise no benefits are conferred.

- •   Novice: You read up on trance states once.
- •• Practiced: You are serious about your self-contemplation and have attained a respectable amount of focus.
- ••• Competent: You have studied under a master.
- •••• Expert: You can find peace even when everything is going to Hell.
- ••••• Master: Yes.

Possessed By: Mystics, New Agers, Martial Artists, Philosophers, Vampires Seeking Golconda

Specialties: Transcendence, Adverse Conditions, Calm and Centering, Problem Analysis

Pilot

"Tower, this is Victor Three-Seven. I say again, we are declaring an in-flight emergency. Our left engine is out, we are losing hydraulic pressure, and we have smoke in the cabin."

"What the hell hit us?" someone screamed from behind the cockpit.

"I don't know! It felt like a bird strike or something, but we're 20,000 feet up, for Christ's sake! Find where that smoke's coming from!"

"What the — two o'clock, low, what the hell is that thing?"

The full moon was briefly eclipsed by immense bat-wings as the creature banked for another attack.

"I don't know, but it's coming back at us. Hang on, I'm going to try to lose it in those thunderheads…."

You can operate air or sea vehicles. Pilot must be bought separately for each vehicle type listed below; a Navy fighter pilot may not know the first thing about how to operate a ferry hovercraft on the English Channel. At the Storyteller's discretion, related Pilot subskills may overlap as if they were two dots lower: A military transport pilot with Pilot Transport/Passenger Aircraft 4 would be able to operate a small business jet as if she had Pilot Business/Commuter Aircraft 2, although using Pilot Cabin Cruiser would be right out of the question. Storytellers should remember, however, that most

vehicles covered by this Skill are vastly more complex than a car, and instrument and control arrangements are more different than similar; just because a Ventrue knows how to sail her privateer, she won't necessarily even know where the helm is on a supertanker.

- • Novice: You can handle the most basic of maneuvers with an instructor at your shoulder.
- •• Practiced: You can perform solo operations on a few models.
- ••• Competent: You are a professional, and can manage smooth, routine trips.
- •••• Expert: A trained combat pilot, exceptional maneuvers are within your grasp.
- ••••• Master: Han Solo, Maverick or Blackbeard.

Possessed By: Professionals, Police and Military Personnel, Enthusiasts

Suggested Air Vehicle Types: Hang Glider, Balloon, Single-Engine Aircraft, Business/Commuter Aircraft, Transport/Passenger Aircraft, Fighter Aircraft, Bomber, Observation/Traffic Helicopter, Passenger/Transport Helicopter, Attack Helicopter

Suggested Watercraft Types: Small Sailboat, Racing Sailboat, Sailing Ship, Swamp Airboat, Inflatable Assault Boat, Small Motorboat, Racing Motorboat, Cabin Cruiser, Yacht, Small Ship, Large Ship, Monstrous Ship, Research Submarine, Hovercraft, Hydrofoil, Personal Watercraft

Specialties: Combat Maneuvers, Takeoff/Landing/Docking, Rough Weather, Tight Quarters/Low Altitude, Specific Model of Vehicle, Instrument-Only (Blind) Operations, Racing

RIDE

Leah risked a glance backward and was nearly brained by a branch for her troubles. "Dammit! I'm lost, I have a dozen of the bastards on my tail, I haven't done this in a hundred years, I don't have a proper saddle, and the beast doesn't even like me."

As if in response to her litany of inconveniences, her horse jerked his head again and tried to turn as gunshots and catcalls sounded in the distance. Leah kicked him in the flanks twice. "No you don't. The border's only 20 miles away, and you're going to get me there, because even if I could find a jeep it wouldn't make it through these mountains. Keep moving."

Whether you come from a time before gasoline engines (or a modern place without them), or you keep in practice as a hobby, you know how to ride an animal without being thrown or falling off. This Skill also reflects your knowledge of such animals and the equipment necessary to ride and your ability to break and train a new mount.

If fighting while mounted, you cannot use more dots in your combat Abilities than you have dots in Ride. For example, if Leah has Melee 2, Ride 3 and Firearms 4 and is caught by her pursuers, she can sword-fight from horse-

back with her full Melee, but may only shoot from the saddle as if she had Firearms 3.

- • Novice: You can stay in the saddle at low speeds.
- •• Practiced: You can manage a gallop and maybe a few fancy-looking tricks at low speeds.
- ••• Competent: You indulge in fox hunting or polo on the weekends.
- •••• Expert: You are a show-jumping champion or professional jockey.
- ••••• Master: You are as comfortable in the saddle as on your own two feet, and can accomplish just about anything with a well-trained mount.

Possessed By: Cowboys, Enthusiasts, Stunt Riders, Elder Kindred, People Who Live in Rural Settings

Specialties: Bareback, Combat, Tricks, Racing, Breaking and Training, Horses, Camels, Mules, Elephants

SLEIGHT OF HAND

Khalil smiled as he bowed and kissed the prince's hand, his cold lips lingering on her skin a moment longer than necessary. "The pleasure, Lady Tinbergen, is entirely mine."

"Ah, my honored guest. Corrie, please."

Actually, *Khalil thought as he slipped her ring into his pocket, I think "fool" has a nice ring to it.*

The speed and deftness of your hands can deceive the eyes of others. You can perform magic tricks, cheat at cards, or pilfer the pockets of unsuspecting bystanders.

- • Novice: Card tricks at cast parties
- •• Practiced: Children's birthday parties
- ••• Competent: Stage magician
- •••• Expert: TV magician or professional pickpocket
- ••••• Master: Prince of Thieves

Possessed By: Thieves, Stage Magicians, Aspiring Casanovas

Specialties: Cards, Pickpocket, "Conjuration," Entertainment, Shoplifting

PROFESSIONAL SKILL

This category encompasses anything that the Storyteller deems to be a taught Ability and is primarily active in application. Storytellers should first examine the list of existing Skills and Secondary Skills to determine if a particular task might fall under one of those (e.g. Tracking would be a specialty of Survival).

- • Novice: You've apprenticed.
- •• Practiced: You have a handle on the basics.

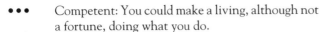

- ••• Competent: You could make a living, although not a fortune, doing what you do.
- •••• Expert: You know the more esoteric uses of your Skill, and are rarely at a loss.
- ••••• Master: You are an acknowledged authority on your chosen field of endeavor.

Suggested Professional Skills: Blacksmith, Cooking, Fast-Draw, Forgery, Game Playing, Gunsmith, Mechanic, Navigation, Torture

KNOWLEDGES
AREA KNOWLEDGE

"How many cops we got back there, brother?" Tyrus asked the two in the back seat.

"Four, maybe five pigs. No bikes — they're all squad cars. "Can you outrun them?"

"Not with y'all motherfuckers weighing us down!" Tyrus snarled. "Anthius, where can we hide around here?"

"Take a right up here; there's an alley on the far side of that pawn shop that's too narrow for them to get through."

The old Dodge groaned in protest as Tyrus threw the car into a hard turn. Garbage and dead cats squelched beneath the tires, and last week's front page of the Chicago Tribune *briefly flattened itself against the windshield. "Where now?"*

Anthius frowned at the street signs as the car shot out into traffic again. "Two blocks down and left, there's an empty office building. We can ditch the car and hide in there…."

You are familiar with the geography and mortal residents and politics of an area, usually a city. This Knowledge does not include Kindred affairs, which are covered by Camarilla and Sabbat Lore and City Secrets, below. It does include nightspots, hiding places, hospitals, gang turf, local celebrities and special events.

- • Student: You've read Fodor's.
- •• College: You may have lived in the area for a couple of years.
- ••• Masters: You've been a resident for a decade or so.
- •••• Doctorate: You're a native and have lived in the region your whole life — or unlife.
- ••••• Scholar: You could write the definitive book on the city, and may have spent several lifetimes there.

Possessed By: Locals, Cops, Tour Guides, City Planners, Reporters

Specialties: History, Geography, Politics, Transportation, Law, Customs, Celebrations

BUREAUCRACY

"You don't understand!" Stephan pounded the ticket agent's desk and waved his press pass in her face one more time. "I didn't change my reservation — I have to be on the 7:35 flight out! It's… it's vitally important that I leave here!"

"I'm sorry, sir," she said without a trace of remorse, "but according to our computers, you did indeed cancel your reservation. If you'll just have a seat, we can put you on the 9:20 to Detroit, where you can change over to an L.A. flight."

Stephan sank almost to his knees, barely steadying himself on the edge of the desk. "You don't understand," he whispered. "They'll be here for me soon…."

Bureaucracy represents your ability to get what you want out of "the system," whether through paperwork, phone calls or bribery. This Knowledge is useful for manipulating city officials, navigating the political system or even operating a bureaucracy of your own design. Those with high Bureaucracy are among the most organized people in existence.

- • Student: You can keep a small company organized.
- •• College: You understand the *real* basics of power structures.
- ••• Masters: You can perform stalling tactics for as long as it takes.
- •••• Doctorate: When you talk, your senator listens.
- ••••• Scholar: When you talk, the IRS listens.

Possessed By: Bankers, Office Workers, Government Employees, Lawyers, Politicians, Journalists

Specialties: Negotiation, Bribery, Diplomacy, Bluffing, Stalling, Government, Military

CAMARILLA LORE

Jan thoughtfully tapped the letter against his thigh as he stared out the window of his study. "You say Prince Lodin sent you personally?"

The messenger bowed. "Yes, Mr. Pieterzoon. He sends his warmest regards."

"Surprising, considering that we never got on well when I passed through Chicago—," Jan turned, fangs bared. "And also considering that he's been dead for six years! Now tell me the truth, whelp, before I lose what little patience your transparent deception has left me!"

You know about the Camarilla. You are familiar with its leaders, both the real ones and the figureheads. You know history, the names of archons and justicars, the decisions of past conclaves, legends, the current "Most Wanted" list and the political stances of the major players. Not all Camarilla members have this Knowledge; many do not concern themselves with the night-to-night affairs of the political entity to which they belong. It is difficult for an outsider to have more than two dots in this Knowledge, and only the best-informed mortals will have even one.

- • Student: What any member would know if she bothered to ask.
- •• College: What most Ventrue know.
- ••• Masters: What most Nosferatu or Tremere know.

- •••• Doctorate: What most princes and archons know.
- ••••• Scholar: What only the justicars and Inner Circle representatives know.

Possessed By: Camarilla Members, Sabbat Spies and Paladins, Wise Members of the Independent Clans

Specialties: History, Legends, Princes, Justicars, High-Level Politics, Laws and Conclave Decisions, Current Affairs

CITY SECRETS

"Sit down, boy." Marsha pulled the unresisting neonate into a chair to punctuate her words. "Time for your lesson on who really runs this place."

The younger Ventrue blinked. "I thought Prince Marcus was in charge. I mean, isn't he always?"

Marsha sighed. "What are they teaching you up north these nights? Honestly, I don't know why the directorate sent you down here. Now pay attention. You see those two plotting over in the corner there? No, don't look right at them!"

The neonate nodded mutely, toying with his cufflinks.

"Those are two of the primogen — the tall, scrawny one's Philip, and the short one who looks like he didn't get any sleep yesterday is Richard. They and the rest of the clan elders really run this city. Marcus hasn't been more than a figurehead for years now. Philip has a special hold on the prince, because last year Marcus' favorite childe got himself in a bit of a mess with the Tremere — never mind how I know that…"

You know *things*. City Secrets is a measure of how much a character knows of the hidden affairs of a city, the local intrigues and power plays and social structures and nightly double-dealings (not necessarily of the Kindred, either — "I remember a priest who said this place was cursed back when they built this building"). City Secrets cannot be acquired during character generation, but only through direct experience. It is suggested that the Storyteller award separate experience points for City Secrets at the end of every game session during which the characters increase their familiarity with the local Kindred world. Information about Kindred affairs in different cities can give a character multiple City Secrets ratings: a Camarilla courier might have City Secrets (Boston) 4, City Secrets (D.C.) 2, and City Secrets (Baltimore) 3 while knowing nothing about the Kindred of New York.

- • Student: A mere childe, not even presented to the prince; you don't even bother to keep up with the local television news.
- •• College: A naïve young leech, you have barely begun your descent; occasionally, you make a connection between appearances and realities.
- ••• Masters: You know what not to do, which can be even more important than what to do.
- •••• Doctorate: You may be an advisor to the mayor or the prince.

- ••••• Scholar: Only the prince and the elder of the local Nosferatu might know more than you.

Possessed By: Kindred, Ghouls, Very Lucky Hunters, Local Reporters

Specialties: Prince/Archbishop, Primogen/Prisci, Coteries/Packs, The Opposition, High Society, Masquerade, Where the Power Lies, Who's Screwing Who, Historical Rivalries, Political Mistakes

CRYPTOGRAPHY

"We just got this from the archbishop. He says it was taken off a Camarilla courier, but we can't read it. Can you make anything out of this?"

Kathryn nodded. "I've seen this before, or something like it. It's a Soviet code scheme from the late '50's, probably straight off a surplus encryption machine. Give me a couple of hours and I should have something for you. Oh, and I'll need another notebook, a dozen pencils and a Russian-English dictionary. No, make that Russian-Spanish. Monçada will want it in his native language."

You are skilled at both creating and breaking codes and ciphers. With an Intelligence + Cryptography roll (base difficulty 7, but harder for extremely complex or technical messages), you can construct a code that can be read only by someone who scores as many successes as you on the same roll. You can also break a code in the same manner. Some codes require specialized equipment and a corresponding level of Computer, and government ciphers may take weeks or may be literally unbreakable.

- • Student: Crossword puzzle master: simple word transpositions and the like
- •• College: Military signals officer: simple mathematical formulae
- ••• Masters: Intelligence analyst: PGP or other commercial ciphers
- •••• Doctorate: CIA cipher specialist: low-security military communications
- ••••• Scholar: The NSA's finest: top-secret burn-before-reading codes

Possessed By: Mathematicians, Computer Programmers, Spies, Military Intelligence Officers, NSA Technicians

Specialties: Data Compression, Specific Nation's Ciphers, Mathematical Encryption, Alphabetical Encryption, Radio Communications, Commercial Protocols

ENIGMAS

"Come now, Kemintiri. Surely there must be some way into your lair. Even you must enter and exit, otherwise it's not much of a lair…."

Hesha studied the small building intently, the light from the moon illuminating nothing on the facade that appeared to hide a portal.

"If this is the 'Devil's Den,' as you claim, how does the Devil come and go? Unless—" Hesha stopped short, smiled to himself and walked around to the rear of the stone edifice. He pressed a small gem into a rough stone socket at the foundation of the building, and the stone slab slid quietly open.

"Of course. The Devil enters and leaves through the back of men's heads at the base of their necks," Hesha chuckled to himself and entered the darkness below him.

Enigmas allows you to pull together information for puzzles of all shapes and sizes. With this Knowledge, you can piece together relevant facts and details and combine them into a coherent whole. Enigmas is also useful for piercing the multiple veils of deception that Kindred and kine alike surround themselves with on a nightly basis.

- • Student: You can put together a large jigsaw puzzle or solve simple riddles from mythology.
- •• College: Magazine logic problems are a snap.
- ••• Masters: Your powers of deduction cast a blinding light on the dark schemes of lesser minds.
- •••• Doctorate: Chaos or conspiracy theories are your mental toys.
- ••••• Scholar: You understand some higher power's designs on the inner workings of the universe.

Possessed By: Sages, Philosophy Professors, Detectives, Intelligence Analysts, Gamers, Metaphysicians, New Age Mystics

Specialties: Riddles, Dream Interpretation, Conspiracies, Quantum Physics, Chaos Theory

RESEARCH

Andrea rubbed her aching eyes and shuffled her notes, trying to make some sense of the night's work. "White eagles, blue canaries, Methuselahs, Malkavians, rowan, ironwood, silk and Toledo steel…. The bastard's true name is in here somewhere, I know it is. If I just didn't have so damn many books to go through! Haven't these people ever heard of CD-ROM?"

Anyone who wants to find a specific piece of information needs this Knowledge. Research and the right materials can help you find almost anything that anyone's ever written down. Many Research projects involve extended rolls and several nights' work, and some things may not be in the most accessible of libraries.

- • Student: You are familiar with public libraries and Web search engines.
- •• College: You may work part-time as a research assistant. You know how to use Gopher and FTP systems, as well as several obscure hardcopy filing methods.
- ••• Masters: You are familiar with some private archives in your areas of study.
- •••• Doctorate: With time, you can find almost anything you need to know.

••••• Scholar: You are virtually a walking cross-reference library, and know where to start looking before the question has been fully phrased.

Possessed By: Professors, Writers, Journalists, Librarians, Detectives, Scholars

Specialties: Online, Arcane and Occult, Oral Traditions, Folklore, Specific Knowledge, Interviews, Speed Reading, Keeping Your Search Quiet

SABBAT LORE

The bonfire flickered, casting deep shadows over the assembled Kindred. "We are gathered here," the pack priest intoned, "to pass judgment on a traitor — a Camarilla spy whom we trusted as one of our blood. Do you have any last words before you are given new form to suit your acts?"

Skeet writhed vainly in the grip of the two paladins who held him. "You bastards! You have no idea who you're dealing with! Just because I don't know all of your secret handshakes and bullshit Texas chupacabra rituals doesn't make me a Camarilla pawn! I serve the Bishop of Detroit, and he'll have your heads on pikes along the fucking interstate!"

The priest whirled suddenly, transfixing Skeet with her icy glare. "You say you serve the Bishop of Detroit? Then you know that three elders of the Black Hand claim that title and battle for it nightly. Which one of them do you serve? Answer truly, and we may yet spare you."

You know about the Sabbat. You know who holds power where, which faction is in ascendance in various areas, where the war against the Camarilla is going well and where it's failing, history, the tenets of various belief systems and the reputations of famous (or infamous) packs. Not all Sabbat members have this Knowledge; the Creation Rites do not always allow time to give new members a detailed briefing. It is almost impossible for an outsider to have more than two dots in this Knowledge, and very few mortals survive long enough to have even one. Sabbat Lore may not be acquired during character creation.

- • Student: What most members who live long enough to ask know.
- •• College: What most pack priests and leaders members know.
- ••• Masters: What most bishops and Lasombra know.
- •••• Doctorate: What the archbishops and paladins know.
- ••••• Scholar: What only the prisci, cardinals and regent know.

Possessed By: Sabbat Members, Camarilla Spies and Archons

Specialties: History, Legends, Leadership, The Sabbat Inquisition, High-Level Politics, Current Affairs, Auctoritas Ritae

Sewer Lore

Matthew splashed through a puddle of something he refused to look at. "Hey, Ramona, are you sure you know where we're going?"

Ramona grunted, "Well, I think so. The Nos said we were supposed to meet them down here, and I think I followed the directions."

"Well, then where are we? I haven't seen any road signs down here!"

"Um… we're… uh…"

"You are lost," interjected a new voice. It was suave, urbane and lightly accented in Italian. "You are confused, you are tired, you are nowhere near your repulsive friends, and you are trespassing in my domain."

"Oops."

You know quite a bit about sewers in general, and are quite familiar with the networks that run under your city of residence. You can navigate through the sewers and sub-basements with reasonable certainty of your directions. You know which territories are claimed by the Nosferatu and Giovanni, and whether or not it is safe to pass through those areas. You also know where other creatures, both normal and supernatural, may exist, and you know how many of the stories about them are rumors and how many are the horrid facts. Theoretically, you could survive underground for quite some time.

- • Student: Teenage runaway
- •• College: City maintenance worker
- ••• Masters: Nosferatu or Giovanni neonate
- •••• Doctorate: Nosferatu guide
- ••••• Scholar: Nosferatu elder

Possessed By: Street People, Nosferatu and Giovanni, some Malkavians and Samedi, Sewer Monsters, Public Works Employees

Specialties: Food, Hiding Places, Shortcuts, Havens, Information, Gathering Places, Staying Clean

Expert Knowledge

Like Hobby Talent and Professional Skill, this is a catchall category. An Expert Knowledge is anything that is primarily intellectual or mental in nature and must be studied. Storytellers should first examine the list of existing Knowledges and Secondary Knowledges to determine if a particular field of expertise might fall under one of those (e.g. Forensics would be a specialty of Investigation).

- • Student: You've taken an undergraduate course or read a few books.
- •• College: You may have minored in the field.
- ••• Masters: You might hold a degree and are well versed in what's been written.
- •••• Doctorate: You are well-versed in what hasn't been written.
- ••••• Scholar: You know the hidden mysteries of your field and are a veritable font of information.

Suggested Expert Knowledges: Archaeology, Engineering (Aerospace, Architectural, Mechanical, etc.), Military Science, Philosophy, Psychology

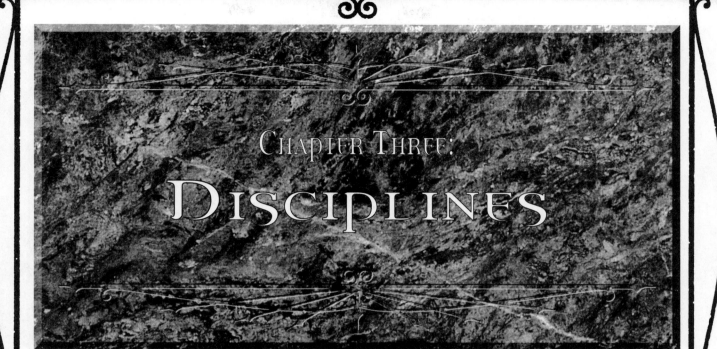

Chapter Three:
Disciplines

Many and varied are the supernatural abilities of the Children of Caine, yet even the most cosmopolitan of Kindred is unlikely to have seen *everything* unlife has to offer. A few bloodlines possess their own unique abilities, stemming from their lands of origin, their mysterious progenitors or even their natures as vampires.

This chapter examines the Disciplines practiced by the bloodlines presented in Chapter One. As mentioned, these vampires are quite rare, and their mystical abilities are proportionately so. Unless a Kindred has dealt with these powers before, there is no reason for a character to have any familiarity with these Disciplines. Storytellers are advised to use the Disciplines, like their parent bloodlines, frugally, to preserve **Vampire's** sense of mystery and malignant wonder. Additionally, most Kindred are loath to reveal their secrets to others of their kind — the vampire of a clan that does not regularly practice these Disciplines and yet commands them must be an interesting character indeed.

Ultimately, these powers are here for your use. They are best implemented as tools of horror and the unknown, not to provide new Traits for characters to stock up on. Like the bloodlines presented earlier, feel free to ignore these powers or disallow players to make use of them. Familiarity breeds contempt, and confronting characters with a mysterious power is more effective if they don't know the ins and outs of its capacities.

Savvy Storytellers may also notice that not every Discipline presented here continues to the ninth level of mastery. This is because not every bloodline has a member of sufficient generation to master the highest levels of the Disciplines. The lowest generation any Daughter of Cacophony is believed to have attained is the sixth, while the Samedi are rumored to have no member below the fifth. Many Kindred even suspect the highest levels of Obeah to have fallen into obscurity, as there are no known Salubri of sufficient generations active in the modern nights. Whether or not any of this is certifiably true, of course, may never be known.

Melpominee

Named for Melpomene, the Greek Muse of tragedy, the unique Discipline of the Daughters of Cacophony is one of speech and song. The powers of this Discipline explore the various uses of the voice for both benefit and harm. As is the case with mortal art, it is not always clear which of those directions these powers take. No character may have a rating in Melpominee higher than her Performance rating. Melpominee affects the subject's soul as well as the ears; thus, it works perfectly well on deaf subjects, and has caused at least one known breach of the Masquerade due to this effect. Additionally, the powers of Melpominee work only on those who are present when it is used — Daughters of Cacophony cannot "encode" Melpominee effects onto compact discs or send them across radio signals.

• The Missing Voice

A vampire with this power may "throw" her voice anywhere within her line of sight, even carrying on two conversations simultaneously (one with her Missing Voice and one with her actual, physical one). Treacherous Daughters of Cacophony impersonate other individuals' voices in order to mislead listeners, and less devious members of the bloodline can use their two voices simultaneously to perform hauntingly beautiful "duets" or eerie one-actress plays.

System: This power functions automatically as long as the character wills it. However, using The Missing Voice while performing any action other than speech or singing incurs a penalty of two dice on that action due to the disruption of the character's concentration.

•• Phantom Speaker

With this power, the vampire may project her voice to any one individual with whom she has more than passing familiarity. The only distance limitation is that it must be night wherever the intended listener is. The vampire can talk, sing or make whatever other noises she wants. The sounds are inaudible to anyone but the intended subject, unless an eavesdropper has Auspex 3 or higher (and has reason to be listening for such). The Kindred cannot hear the sounds — or the subject's responses — unless she is within earshot. The use of Phantom Speaker has been responsible for several cases of "paranoid schizophrenia."

System: The player rolls Wits + Performance (difficulty 7) and spends a blood point. Each success allows one turn of speech; three or more successes allow speech for an entire scene.

••• Madrigal

The Kindred may imbue her audience with the emotions expressed in her song, rousing them to passion or deluging them with seemingly bottomless despair. Princes on good terms with Daughters of Cacophony sometimes have the songstresses croon before they make an appearance, bolstering their fellow Kindred with a sense of loyalty.

System: The player rolls Charisma + Performance (difficulty 7). Each success instills the chosen emotion in a fifth of the Kindred's audience (more than five successes have no additional effect). The Storyteller decides precisely which members of the audience are affected. Characters may resist this power for the duration of the scene with the expenditure of a Willpower point, but only if they have reason to believe that they are being controlled by outside individuals. The song the vampire sings must also reflect the emotion she wishes to engender — no one's going to mob the concert security no matter how well she sings "High Hopes," but they might if she wails "Cop-killer."

Affected individuals should act in accordance with their Natures — enraged Conformists would join a riot but not start one, aroused Bravos may force their attentions on the object of their desire, and jealous Directors may send cronies after their rivals.

•••• Siren's Beckoning

This power reaches deep into its victims' souls to twist their psyches. Siren's Beckoning causes temporary insanity in its victims. Malkavians and vampires in Golconda are immune to Siren's Beckoning; the former are too warped to be further affected, and the latter are too centered. Siren's Beckoning can affect only one victim at a time.

System: Siren's Beckoning requires an extended, resisted roll. The player rolls Manipulation + Performance (difficulty of the target's Willpower); the victim resists by rolling Willpower (difficulty of the singer's Appearance + Performance). If the singer accumulates five more successes than the victim at any point, the hapless soul acquires a new derangement (or Psychological Flaw) of the Storyteller's choice. This derangement normally lasts for one night per success over five. With a total of 20 net successes, the Daughter can make it permanent.

••••• Virtuosa

Although many low-level Melpominee powers allow a vampire to affect only one target at a time, those who have mastered the Discipline may entertain a wider audience, as it were.

System: The Daughter may use Phantom Speaker or Siren's Beckoning on a number of targets equal to her Stamina + Performance. The player must spend one blood point for every five targets beyond the first to be affected in such a manner.

•••••• Shattering Crescendo

Mortal singers can shatter wineglasses with their voices by finding the precise pitch at which the glass resonates. A talented Daughter of Cacophony can go beyond the destruction of relatively fragile objects, pitching her voice to find the resonant frequency of virtually any object, including a human or Kindred body. Only one victim at a time can be affected by Shattering Crescendo; anyone else within earshot will hear a piercing, though not harmful, shriek.

System: Use of this power requires that the victim be within hearing range (characters with hearing difficulties — or Heightened Senses — are affected at the same range as other victims). The player spends one blood point and rolls Manipulation + Performance (difficulty of the target's Stamina + Fortitude). Each success inflicts one health level of aggravated damage. If using this power on an inanimate object, the Storyteller determines how many dice (if any) with which the object may "soak" and how many successes are needed to completely shatter it.

••••••• Persistent Echo

With this power, the Daughter can speak or sing to the air and leave her words for a later listener. This can be either the next being to stand where the character is when she uses this power or a specific individual that she is already acquainted with. Persistent Echo can also be used to "suspend" other Melpominee powers for a future listener or victim.

System: The player rolls Stamina + Performance (difficulty 8) and spends a blood point. Each success yields one turn of speech that may be left to be heard later. If the player wishes to time-delay another Melpominee power, the roll for that power must be made at +1 difficulty. The echo stays suspended for a maximum number of nights equal to twice the vampire's Stamina + Performance before fading.

The Kindred may choose to make the echo audible to anyone who stands in her position for the duration of the power — in effect, an endlessly looped mystic recording. Conversely, she may choose for it to fade away once it is heard for the first time. She may also choose to leave it dormant until activated by the presence of a specific individual with whom she is familiar. If the echo is made a one-time-only effect, all traces of the power disappear once the vampire's words echo to the intended recipient.

If a character uses Heightened Senses in an area where an "unactivated" echo exists, he will hear a faint murmur. Three successes on a Perception + Occult roll (difficulty 8) are necessary to hear the message, and a botch on this roll will deafen the listener for the rest of the night.

Obeah

Although most modern Kindred who have heard of the Salubri know of them as soul-stealing abominations who should be reported to the prince, some elders still remember Saulot's line as a double-edged blade, gentle healers on one hand and matchless holy warriors on the other. Some Kindred have reported dealing with a Salubri who possesses frightening martial prowess. Whether or not this is the result of an atavism of this Discipline or an entirely separate power is unknown.

The characteristic third eye of the Salubri appears around the time that any vampire, regardless of clan or bloodline, develops the second level of Obeah. The eye opens whenever any power of second level or higher is used. The Salubri give no concrete answer as to how or why this occurs. The most common theory is that the eye serves as a conduit for spiritual energies, both sensing and emitting them.

• Sense Vitality

The Salubri can feel the flow of a subject's life force after touching him. Sense Vitality may be used to determine how much damage a person can withstand before death, which can be useful in sizing up a potential opponent. It can also aid in medical diagnosis or feeding, as it can reveal infections and diseases.

System: The Salubri must touch the target to see how close to death she is. This also requires a Perception + Empathy roll (difficulty 7). One success on this roll identifies a subject as a mortal, vampire, ghoul or other creature, or none of the above. Two successes reveal how many health levels of damage the subject has suffered. Three successes tell how full the subject's blood pool is (if a vampire) or how many blood points she has left in her system (if a mortal or other blood-bearing form of life). Four successes reveal any diseases in the subject's bloodstream, such as hemophilia or HIV. A player may opt to learn the information yielded by a lesser degree of success — for example, a player who accumulates three successes may learn whether or not a subject is a vampire as well as the contents of his blood pool.

Alternately, this power may be used as a sort of limited "aftersight," revealing to the Salubri how the subject came to be in her current state. Each success on this roll allows the player to ask the Storyteller one question about the subject's health or health levels. "Was he drugged?" or "Are his wounds aggravated?" are valid questions, but "Did the Sabbat do this?" or "What did the Lupine who killed him look like?" are not. The Salubri may use this power on herself if she has injuries but has somehow lost the memory of how the wounds were received.

•• Anesthetic Touch

This power may be used to block a voluntary subject's pain from wounds or disease, or to put a mortal to sleep. As with Sense Vitality, physical contact is required to anesthetize someone. This power may not be used to block the Salubri's own pain.

System: If the subject is willing to undergo this process, the player needs to spend a blood point to block the subject's pain and make a Willpower roll (difficulty 6). This allows the subject to ignore all wound penalties for one turn per success. A second application of this power may be made once the first one has expired, at the cost of another blood point and another Willpower roll. If the subject is unwilling for some reason, the player must make a contested Willpower roll against the subject (difficulty 8).

To put a mortal to sleep, the same system applies. The mortal sleeps for five to 10 hours — whatever his normal sleep cycle is — and regains one temporary Willpower point upon awakening. He sleeps peacefully and does not suffer nightmares or the effects of any Derangements while asleep. He may be awakened normally (or violently).

Kindred are unaffected by this power — their corpselike bodies are too tied to death.

••• Corpore Sano

The Salubri may heal the injuries of others by laying his hands over the wound and channeling his own energies into the healing process. The subject feels a warm tingling in the affected area as it heals.

System: This power works on any living or undead creature, but the character must touch the actual injury (or the closest part of the victim's body in the case of internal injuries). Each health level to be healed requires the expenditure of one blood point and one turn of contact. Aggravated wounds may also be healed in this manner, but the vampire must spend two blood points instead of one for an aggravated health level.

•••• Mens Sana

This power allows the Salubri to remove a subject's derangements, or to at least mitigate their effects for a time. Salubri Embraced in the modern age sometimes prefer to use psychological interview techniques, while older members of the bloodline prefer to whisper soothing words or perform exorcism rituals. Some Kindred scholars believe the Antediluvian Saulot eased the Ancient Malkav's madness with this power, but a few others believe that Saulot may have caused Malkav's madness himself....

System: The player spends two blood points and rolls Intelligence + Empathy (difficulty 8). The use of Mens Sana takes at least 10 minutes of relatively uninterrupted conversation. Success cures the subject of one derangement of the Salubri player's choice. This power cannot cure a Malkavian of his core derangement, though it temporarily alleviates its effects for the rest of the scene. A botch inflicts the same derangement on the Salubri for the rest of the scene, and the target's own derangement is intensified. This power may not be used by the Salubri to cure her own derangements.

• • • • • Unburdening the Bestial Soul

The mainstay of the healing abilities of the Salubri, this power allows a character to stare into another individual's eyes and draw the subject's soul out of his body and into the Salubri's third eye, storing it within the Salubri's own soul while working powerful healing magics on it

This power is the justification that the Tremere give for their pursuit of the Salubri as "soul-stealing fiends." Tremere accounts of the diabolical practices of the Salubri ensure that few subjects are willing to have their souls removed from their bodies.

The subject's body becomes a mindless husk while it lacks a soul, and may not be affected by any mind-altering Disciplines or other supernatural powers — there's no mind there to control. However, it does respond to simple verbal commands from the Salubri who has its soul. If not reminded to eat or perform other personal upkeep, the body will not do so and will eventually die.

System: This power may be used to draw out the soul of any character *except* those with Humanity or Path ratings of 1 or 0 or those who follow particularly inhuman Paths of Enlightenment; some souls are beyond redemption. The player rolls Stamina + Empathy (difficulty of 12 minus the subject's Humanity or Path rating). A botch gives the Salubri the subject's Derangement for the remainder of the scene. The Salubri must make eye contact with the subject and the subject must be willing to be subjected to this power.

A soul drawn out in this manner becomes part of the Salubri's while the healing process takes place. She may return it to its proper body at any time. While the soul is within the Salubri, she may spend a permanent Willpower point to restore a point to the subject's Humanity or Path rating. The Salubri may restore a maximum number of points equal to her Empathy score, and may not raise the subject's Humanity or Path higher than the sum of his relevant Virtues (for example, a character subscribing to Humanity with Conscience 3 and Self-Control 3 could not have his Humanity raised above 6 in this manner).

While a soul is being held by the Salubri, its body is an empty husk, comatose or in torpor, with no motivating force within it. A soul whose body is killed immediately vanishes, its disposition unknown to any (although the Salubri strongly suspect that souls that vanish in this manner are completely and irreversibly destroyed). Killing the body of a drawn-out soul may warrant a Conscience or Conviction roll if the killer knows of the soul's absence, at the Storyteller's discretion. There's just no call for such brutality.

A soul that is being detained against its will may attempt to break free from the Salubri. This is resolved by a contested Willpower roll with the Salubri (difficulty of the opponent's Wits + Empathy). Only one attempt per night may be made.

• • • • • • RENEWED VIGOR

The Salubri who has developed this power has heightened his healing abilities to such a degree that he can heal virtually any ailment as long as the subject still lives. All that is required is a touch and a brief moment of concentration.

System: The character touches the individual to be healed and spends a full turn concentrating. The player spends one Willpower point. At the end of the turn, the subject heals *all* lost health levels, including aggravated wounds. If physical contact is not maintained for the entire turn, or if the Salubri is forced to take any action other than concentrating on healing, the Willpower point is lost with no effect on the subject of the healing. The Salubri may use this power on himself.

• • • • • • • SAFE PASSAGE

The Salubri may use this power to pass through a crowd without fear of harm. This is not a power that makes the vampire "invisible to the mind" as Obfuscate does, but rather a sort of "active neutrality" that makes all around the vampire inclined to treat her favorably and step out of her way. She seems inoffensive, pleasant and harmless, and people are respectful and helpful to her without stopping to consider why. This power also ensures that anyone who pursues the vampire or obviously wishes to do her harm is met with unfavorable reactions by those who have been affected by Safe Passage.

System: The Salubri may choose to "turn off" this power, but it is always in effect otherwise. If someone who wishes to harm the Salubri is in a crowd, the vampire and pursuer must make a contested Willpower roll (difficulty 6). If the Salubri wins, the pursuer loses interest in the chase ("Why am I bothering with this when I could be at home, safe, watching MTV?") and loses a number of dice from his dice pools equal to the Salubri's net successes while pursuing her. If the pursuer wins, he is unaffected by the attempt.

If the Salubri is actively seeking shelter or assistance ("Excuse me, sir, can you tell me the best way to the airport from here?"), the player rolls Charisma + Empathy (difficulty 7). Each success reduces the difficulty of a subsequent, appropriate Social roll by one. This affects only attempts to gain seemingly harmless or innocent assistance, such as a place to stay or advice on the bad parts of town — a Salubri won't be able to get automatic weapons or low-grade heroin any easier with this power.

The effects of this power last until the next sunrise. Safe Passage affects only those who know the Salubri casually or not at all. Anyone who has known her long enough to form an opinion of her cannot be touched by this power.

●●●●● ●●● Purification

This power can be used to cleanse a person, item or place of demonic or malign spiritual influence. It is of paramount importance that the Salubri be of strong conviction and moral character, as he pits the purity of his own soul against the corruption he is trying to purge. This power can be used against demonic possession or infernalism, those insidious temptations among debased or power-hungry Kindred, but the price of failure is the Salubri's own soul.

System: This power may be developed and used only by a character with a Humanity or Path rating of 8 or higher. The player spends a Willpower point if the subject is willing and the corrupting agent does not resist (a rare occurrence). If the subject is possessed by a conscious entity, the demon (or other foreign consciousness) fights the Salubri for dominance. This takes place via an extended, contested roll of the Salubri's Humanity or Path versus the opponent's Willpower (each party's difficulty is the other's permanent Willpower). The winner is the first one to have three net successes more than the other. If the player fails, the attempt at purification also fails. If the player botches, the demon takes over the Salubri's body. Purification cannot be used on oneself and has no effect on the Beast or an alternate personality.

Once the initial removal has been successfully performed, the player spends a second Willpower point. The Salubri thrusts the demon into a nearby item, animal or person, trapping the demon in the selected vessel. This must be accomplished within two turns of the Purification and the target must be within physical reach. If this cannot be accomplished, the demon is likely to go free… or find another suitable vessel of its choice (such as the Salubri). If the vampire places the demon in a being who is likely to suffer from its presence, the player must make an immediate Conscience roll (difficulty 8) if the Storyteller believes that the character's morality would object. A botch, in addition to the normal consequences, releases the demon into the world.

●●●●● ●●●● Unbind the Flesh-Clad Soul

The Salubri have always had a unique understanding of the nature of the soul. Some few Salubri elders may bestow (or inflict) upon others the fruits of that understanding. A willing subject may be permanently released from (or locked out of) her body to become a free-roaming soul upon the astral plane, empowered to explore the world (or cursed to wander) for all eternity without the constraints (or benefices) of physical existence. The possibilities inherent to this power are extremely unnerving to the few Tremere who are aware of its existence.

System: The vampire and a willing subject must both enter a deep meditative trance for a minimum of an uninterrupted hour as the Salubri performs the ritual necessary to separate soul from flesh without damaging either. During this period, the player spends a number of blood points equal to twice the permanent Willpower of the subject. At the end of the ritual, the subject's body slips into a coma and dies by the end of the night. Many Tremere and other cautious Kindred warn that the Salubri may misrepresent themselves and convince others to volunteer for a "release" from mortal concerns, when in truth they wish to trap the soul in another plane of existence.

The subject's soul is released from her body and enters the astral plane (see Auspex: Psychic Projection). This separation is permanent and irreversible. The subject is treated as an astrally projecting character in terms of rules mechanics. However, she no longer has a silver cord and no longer needs one, as she exists independently of her body. If she is reduced to zero Willpower through astral combat, she loses one point of permanent Willpower and re-forms after a year and a day at the place where this power was used upon her. A character reduced to zero permanent Willpower is destroyed forever.

This power may only be used upon mortals (excluding mages) and vampires who are in Golconda, and the subject must have a full understanding of what this ritual entails — including its permanence and the impossibility of a reversal. The body of a vampire who is Unbound decays at sunrise. It is possible to drink the blood remaining in the vampire's body, but no benefits are gained from an attempt at diablerie. Any attempt to Embrace the body of an Unbound mortal automatically fails.

The Salubri may use this power on herself, provided she is in Golconda.

THANATOSIS

This Discipline is an exclusive development of the Samedi bloodline, and it is tied intrinsically to the Stiffs' identity and history. Although Thanatosis appears to deal closely with death and the energies of decay, no Giovanni have ever claimed mastery of this power. The clan would undoubtedly be most interested in learning this Discipline. However, the Giovanni view the Samedi with distrust and loathing, while the Samedi take on the Giovanni is usually expressed by muttering a curse on the clan and spitting blood. Thus, the possibility of an exchange of information approaches nil.

• HAGS' WRINKLES

The character can expand or contract her skin and the outer layer of fatty tissue that underlies it. This can be used to change the character's general appearance or to create pockets like a kangaroo's pouch for the concealment of small objects. This power is most effective when used by characters whose skin condition is already deteriorating, as additional distortion is less likely to be visible. If a character other than a Samedi or Nosferatu uses this power, large wrinkles or bulges may be readily visible in her skin.

System: This power requires one turn to shape the wrinkles and the expenditure of a blood point. If the power is used to distort a character's features, the Samedi player must roll Stamina + Acting (difficulty 8, or 7 if the Secondary Skill: Disguise is substituted for Acting). Success raises the difficulty to visually identify the character by one and lasts for one hour per success rolled. If the character is attempting to hide a small object (a wallet, a letter, a small pistol), the roll and duration are the same, but all rolls made to see if the object is detected (for example, a pat-down search or a security guard's visual inspection) are at +2 difficulty.

•• PUTREFACTION

This power allows the character to cause supernaturally rapid decomposition in a living or undead target. The victim loses skin and hair, teeth loosen, blisters and cysts appear, and fungus develops. Needless to say, the psychological impact of this power can be as devastating as the physical.

System: This power first requires that the character touch his intended target. The player then rolls Dexterity + Medicine (difficulty of the target's Stamina + Fortitude) and spends a blood point. Success inflicts one health level of lethal damage on the target and removes

one point of the victim's Appearance. This Appearance loss returns to vampires at the rate of one point per night, but is permanent for mortals (though plastic surgery can correct mortals' physical disfigurement). If a mortal suffers three or more health levels of damage from repeated uses of this power in one scene, gangrene or other ailments may occur.

This power can also be used on plants, in which case the target becomes blighted and withered. It cannot, however, be used on inanimate objects such as cars or wooden stakes.

••• Ashes to Ashes

Ashes to Ashes allows the character to transform herself into a thick, sticky powder, about a double handful in volume (what would be left after a cremation). The character takes no damage from sunlight or flames while in this form, and most physical attacks are ineffectual. However, the character is only dimly cognizant of her surroundings while in ash form, and separation of the ashes can prove catastrophic when the Samedi tries to reform.

System: The transformation to ashes requires one turn and the expenditure of two blood points. While the character is in ash form, the player must make a Perception + Alertness roll (difficulty 9) for any scene in which she wishes her character to be aware of her surroundings. Reforming from the heap of ashes takes one turn. If the character is in a confined space (such as an urn), she explodes from it in a suitably dramatic manner as she brings herself back to full size.

If a Samedi is scattered while in this form, one health level and one blood point are lost for each tenth (roughly) of the character that has been dissipated. Five blood points are required to heal each health level lost in this manner. At the Storyteller's discretion, the Samedi may be missing limbs or vital organs (though never the head or the heart) until the missing health levels are healed.

•••• Withering

Many vampires, accustomed to their forms remaining ageless, have been aghast to discover the effects of this power. Withering allows the Samedi to shrink and warp a victim's limbs, rendering them immobile and causing extreme pain. Some particularly vicious Samedi take shrunken parts of their opponents as trophies or for use in ritual magic.

System: The Samedi must touch the limb he intends to shrivel. The player spends a Willpower point and rolls Manipulation + Medicine (difficulty of the victim's Stamina + Fortitude). Three successes are required for this power to shrink a limb. With one or two successes,

the victim takes one health level of bashing damage, which may be soaked normally, but is otherwise unaffected. (If the Withering attempt is successful, the subject suffers no health level of damage, but rather the withering of the limb itself.) The effects of Withering fade after one night if a vampire or other supernatural creature is the victim, but mortals (including mages) are permanently afflicted unless some type of supernatural healing is used.

If this power is used on an arm or leg, the limb instantly becomes useless. If this power is used on an opponent's head, mortal victims die instantly. Kindred lose two points from all Mental Attributes while their heads are shrunken and are unable to use any Disciplines except Celerity, Potence, and Fortitude. Multiple uses of this power on the same appendage have no additional effect.

••••• Necrosis

Although its effects appear similar to those of Putrefaction, the impact of Necrosis on affected characters is much greater. Necrosis causes living (or undead) tissue to decompose and slough off, exposing bones and organs and leaving the victim open to infection.

System: The Samedi must make contact with the victim. The player spends two blood points and rolls Dexterity + Medicine (difficulty of the target's Stamina + Fortitude). The victim takes a number of health levels of lethal damage equal to the number of successes rolled and suffers additional effects as listed below.

1 success	No additional effects
2 successes	Lose a point of Appearance
3 successes	Lose a point each of Appearance and Dexterity
4 successes	Lose a point each of Appearance, Dexterity, and Strength
5+ successes	Lose two points of Appearance and one each of Dexterity and Strength

Attributes lost in this manner are regained when all damage from the Necrosis attack is healed. If a victim is reduced to zero Strength or Dexterity, he is unable to move except for weak flailing and crawling but may still use Disciplines and spend blood points normally.

•••••• Creeping Infection

Putrefaction, Withering and Necrosis normally take effect instantly. Some elder Samedi have developed such control over these powers that they can delay the eruption of infections and spontaneous decomposition until they are well away from their victims. Mercenary Stiffs are suspected to apply this power with a handshake to give themselves insurance in the event that a "partner" refuses to honor a deal.

System: The player must successfully roll for a use of Putrefaction, Withering or Necrosis, as above, and may delay the effect for a number of months equal to the Samedi's Stamina. The player may spend a blood point at any time during this period in order to activate the dormant power. If the Creeping Infection is not used before the end of its duration, it fades away with no effect.

•••••• • Dust to Dust

This power allows a character in ash form (see Ashes to Ashes, above) to maintain both cohesion and consciousness, as well allowing him limited movement. While adopting the form of a pile of dust may not seem to be a wise tactical decision, enough elder Samedi have found creative uses for this power that it is still taught.

System: While a pile of ash, the Samedi remains fully conscious and may use any Discipline powers that being a pile of dust would permit (Command the Wearied Mind, for instance, is rather difficult to employ without eyes, but Majesty will make the pile of dust very impressive and no maid in her right mind would dare sweep it up). The character cannot be blown apart by high winds, and any deliberate attempt to separate the pile of ash may be resisted with the character's combined Strength, Stamina, Potence and Fortitude. The character may move voluntarily at a speed no higher than that at which a pile of normal dust would be blown by the wind, even if he is indoors. He does not have to move in the direction of the prevailing air currents, and may "flatten" himself by spreading his ashes thinly so as to slip under doors and through cracks. This power functions like Ashes to Ashes in all other respects.

•••••• •• Putrescent Servitude

Although the Samedi are not the only Kindred who are responsible for the creation of zombies, this power allows them to both raise the bodies of the recently dead *and* enslave mortals who are still alive. Corpses animated through this power appear as they did at the time they were raised, which is to say, pale and decayed. Mortals affected by this power gain much the same appearance, although they are generally more intact than their formerly corpse counterparts. Zombies created through this power are unable to speak, think with cognizance, or move at more than a slow trot, but are extremely strong and resilient.

System: The first application of this power allows the Samedi to feed some of her blood to a recently dead corpse (maximum time since death equal to the Samedi's Stamina in weeks) in order to animate it. Three blood points must be spent to bring the corpse back to a semblance of life. A reanimated corpse has the same Physical Attributes as it did in life. It is capable of limited reasoning (reduce all Mental Attributes by one), but free thought is beyond it and the only person it can clearly understand is its master or an individual who its master has directed it to obey. Reanimated corpses possess two levels of Fortitude and three extra health levels. They suffer no dice pool penalties from wounds until they lose their last health level, at which point they collapse and cannot be reanimated again.

A reanimated corpse crumbles to dust at the third sunrise after its creation. Its "lifespan" can be extended by feeding it more blood when it is created — one blood point per extra night.

This power can also be used on a mortal. The Samedi creates a ghoul in the normal fashion, by feeding the subject one blood point. The player then rolls Manipulation + Medicine (difficulty of the mortal's Willpower). Three or more successes are required to turn the mortal into a zombie. If this roll succeeds, the mortal loses all free will, becoming completely subjugated to the Samedi's command. The mortal may try to break free once per night by rolling his permanent Willpower (difficulty of the Samedi's Manipulation + Leadership). If the mortal frees himself, he is still considered a ghoul but regains his free will and normal Mental and Social Attributes (see below). A mortal who botches his Willpower roll or who becomes blood bound to the Samedi may never again attempt to break free.

A mortal under the influence of Putrescent Servitude becomes pale and corpselike. He loses one point from all Social and Mental Attributes (to a minimum value of one). He gains three extra health levels and takes no dice pool penalties from injuries until he reaches Incapacitated, at which point he collapses. One more wound will kill him once he reaches this point. The mortal also gains one level of Potence, as a normal ghoul would, and has the potential to learn other Disciplines if the Samedi feels inclined to teach him.

A ghoul zombie who goes a month without vampiric blood loses all benefits of being a ghoul, as would normally occur. He also loses all effects of this power and regains his free will, though he may still be blood bound to his master.

Chapter Four:
Equipment

FIREARMS

No roleplaying game is complete without a list of entertaining toys from which players may equip their characters. However, every game designer has to determine where between "minimal" and "exhaustive" the list will fall. Thus, this section mainly covers equipment that requires Traits, such as weapons. Commonplace things such as camping equipment and new fashions can be priced easily at your local mall. Other items can be found in catalogs from companies such as U.S. Cavalry or The Sharper Image. As always, the Golden Rule applies: If you know more about a particular item than we present here, feel free to modify its numbers accordingly, or cut it altogether if you don't like it.

One thing to bear in mind with equipment of this nature is that most of it is either outright illegal or highly restricted. Don't be shy about telling a player "no" if she comes up with some cockeyed plan to arm her coterie with .50-caliber machine guns. **Vampire** is a horror game, not an action movie.

This section is intended to provide a fairly comprehensive selection of weapons that might find their way into the hands of a character, or be used against said character by various opponents. It is by no means a complete index of all weapons in use in the world today. Should the player or Storyteller desire a more in-depth look at guns, there are many books on the market devoted to them.

Most nations have rather restrictive laws concerning the possession of fully automatic weapons, and handguns and sporting weapons are falling under tighter and tighter control. Even in the World of Darkness, it is difficult to acquire automatic weapons without black market connections or a valid collector's permit, and any use of such firearms in a city will almost certainly draw some degree of police attention. Storytellers should feel perfectly justified in making both the use and acquisition of such guns more trouble than it is worth for characters.

Firearm Traits

Caliber: The diameter of the bullet fired by the gun in question. Caliber is given in either a fraction of an inch (e.g. .45 caliber is 45/100 of an inch across) or millimeters (e.g. 9mm), with the exception of shotgun rounds, which are measured in gauge.

Damage: The base number of dice rolled for damage after a successful strike. All firearms do lethal damage against mortal targets. Against vampires, firearms do merely bashing damage, unless the head is targeted (which adds two to attack difficulties and one die to damage pools, as per **Vampire: The Masquerade**, page 212), in which case the damage is considered lethal.

Range: This is the practical shot range in yards. Weapons may be fired at twice this distance, but the attacks are considered long range (difficulty 8).

Rate: The gun's maximum cyclic rate, or the number of shots or three-round bursts it may fire per combat turn. This rate does not apply to full-auto or spray attacks.

Clip: The number of shots that the weapon holds. Automatic pistols, submachine guns and any rifle which is described as "automatic" or "semiautomatic" may be carried with one additional round in the firing chamber.

Conceal: P = Can be carried in the pocket; J = Can be hidden in a jacket; T = Can be hidden in a trenchcoat; N = Cannot be concealed on the person at all.

* Indicates the weapon is capable of three-round bursts, full-auto and sprays.

Revolvers

Revolvers are handguns that operate around a cylinder containing five or more rounds. They are generally more bulky than automatic pistols, but are less likely to become inoperable if they malfunction due to their relatively simpler construction. In game terms, this means that most botches with a revolver result in either a misfire (the round doesn't go off) or a shot going into a friend rather than the gun jamming or blowing up. Almost all modern revolvers are double-action, meaning that each pull of the trigger both fires the weapon and rotates a new round into place. Many older models (such as the Colt Peacemaker of American frontier fame) and some newer ones of very high caliber are single-action; this requires the firer to manually cock the hammer between shots, thus vastly reducing the rate of fire. Contrary to what some films have shown, it is impossible to silence a revolver.

Saturday Night Special: This is a catch-all term for any cheap, small-caliber revolver. The majority of crimes involving firearms are committed using these guns. Models are too numerous to list. The two main drawbacks of Saturday night specials are low stopping power and unreliability. However, they are easy to acquire on the street on short notice, ammunition is cheap, and they aren't as big of an investment and therefore are easier to throw away on the run.

Caliber: varies; the most common are .22, .25, and .38 Special

Damage: 3 or 4

Range: 10 to 15

Rate: 3

Clip: 5 , 6, or 8

Conceal: P

Smith & Wesson M640 and Colt Agent: These are representative of small "holdout" revolvers or "detective's specials." They are constructed with a rounded-off hammer to aid in rapid draws from concealment.

Caliber: .38 Special

Damage: 4

Range: 12

Rate: 3

Clip: 6

Conceal: P

Smith & Wesson M686 and Colt Python: Both of these pistols are well-designed mid-caliber revolvers with excellent reputations. These and similar models have seen widespread use among police forces in the past, though revolvers have been replaced almost completely by automatics in modern nights. Most revolvers like these come in a variety of barrel lengths, which have no effect on game play unless the Storyteller wants to tinker with the Range Trait.

Caliber: .357 Magnum

Damage: 5

Range: 30

Rate: 2

Clip: 6

Conceal: J

Smith & Wesson Model 29 and Colt Anaconda: These are a high-caliber revolvers used primarily for hunting and sport-target shooting. Few police departments adopted .44 Magnum weapons, as the heavier caliber pistols are harder to control and are more intimidating than police public relations would like. Characters with Strengths of less than 3 may have difficulty firing these weapons one-handed, at the Storyteller's discretion.

Caliber: .44 Magnum

Damage: 6

Range: 35

Rate: 2

Clip: 6

Conceal: J

Ruger Redhawk: The Redhawk is a massive, brutal revolver, used primarily for hunting. A larger version with a longer barrel, the Super Redhawk, comes with a sling and scope. Both versions are too bulky to be fired one-handed by any character with a Strength of less than 4.

Caliber: .44 Magnum
Damage: 6
Range: 50, 100 for Super Redhawk
Rate: 2
Clip: 6
Conceal: T

Freedom Arms Casull: This weapon, named after its manufacturer, is custom-built on the frame of a Ruger Redhawk and is chambered for ammunition that is a modified rifle round. It is used primarily for hunting bear, moose and other large game, and can mount scopes. As with the Redhawk, it is impossible for a character with Strength of less than 4 to fire a Casull one-handed. A Casull is single-action, which has no game effect other than a relatively lower Rate and an intimidating pause as a character thumbs the hammer back. The expensive custom manufacturing required for a Casull makes it very difficult for a character with less than Resources 3 to acquire one.

Caliber: .454 Casull
Damage: 7
Rate: 1
Range: 40
Clip: 5
Conceal: T

Remington XP-100: Although not a revolver, this pistol is included here for the sake of simplicity. It and its relatives are single-shot, bolt-action pistols made for precise target shooting. Obviously, this means that the precision in question can be put to other uses by an enterprising character. The XP-100 is something of a sniper's weapon in a pistol size. It can mount a scope.

Caliber: .221
Damage: 5
Range: 50
Rate: 1
Clip: 1
Conceal: J

AUTOMATIC PISTOLS:

The term *automatic pistol* is something of a misnomer, as *automatic weapon* has come to be synonymous with "fully automatic." Automatic pistols are more properly referred to as autoloaders, which means that they feed from an internal magazine and use part of the recoil when firing to load the next round into the chamber. Although many autoloaders are manufactured with magazines holding 15 or more rounds, recent American legislation requires all new autoloaders to be sold with magazines holding 10 rounds or less. Autoloaders are more likely to malfunction than revolvers due to their higher complexity (botches are more likely to result in a broken or jammed weapon), but are more commonly used because of their higher rates of fire, higher capacities and lower reload times. Autoloaders can be carried with a full magazine plus a round in the chamber ready to fire. The Clip Traits below apply to full magazines and empty chambers; the +1 indicates that they may be carried with a round in the chamber (though having a round in the chamber makes the weapon much more likely to fire if dropped).

Hammerli M280 Target: As with the Remington XP-100, the Hammerli M280 is a specialized target-shooting pistol. However, most M280s are made with ergonomic grips fitted to the hands of one specific user. In game terms, this adds one die to the Firearms dice pool of the intended user, but anyone else trying to use the weapon *loses* one die. This feature is available on most pistols, but the M280 is one of the few weapons on which it is standard. The M280 can mount a scope.

Caliber: .22 Long Rifle

Damage: 4

Range: 30

Rate: 5

Clip: 5+1

Conceal: J

Sites M380: Manufactured in Italy, this slim and streamlined autoloader is intended for sale to people with minimal weapons training who feel the need to carry an easy-to-hide gun. It is designed for ease of use and maximum concealment. Two other functionally identical versions exist, the M9 and the M40, which fire 9mm and .40 caliber S&W ammunition respectively.

Caliber: .380 Automatic (9mm for M9, .40 S&W for M40)

Damage: 4 (5 for M40)

Range: 20

Rate: 4

Clip: 8+1 (9+1 for M9 and M40)

Conceal: P

Walther PPK: This German-made pistol is familiar worldwide as the signature weapon of James Bond. Although it lacks the punch of larger-caliber weapons, it is small enough to be easily hidden in an ankle holster or similar arrangement. Due to the widespread use of a silencer in the Bond films, it is relatively easy (though still very illegal, without proper permits) to get one for this pistol.

Caliber: .380 Automatic

Damage: 4

Range: 15

Rate: 3

Clip: 7+1

Conceal: P

Beretta Model 92: Made in Italy, this weapon is the most commonly used pistol in American police departments. It was also adopted in the early 1980s as the M9, the official service sidearm of the U.S. Army (though many service personnel still swear by their M1911s). The Model 92 is fairly representative of many high-capacity 9mm autoloaders, such as the Ruger P85 (Antonio Banderas' weapon of choice in *Desperado*), the Browning High-Power (with a 13-round magazine) and the Smith & Wesson 5900 series (the former service sidearm of the FBI), which are all identical to the Model 92 for game purposes.

Caliber: 9mm

Damage: 4

Range: 20

Rate: 4

Clip: 15+1

Conceal: J

Range: 20

Calico Model 950: Looking more like a science-fiction weapon than a traditional pistol, the Calico 950 is nevertheless a very effective weapon. It feeds from a high-capacity cylindrical magazine that locks onto the top of the weapon, parallel to the barrel, rather than sliding into the grip as most autoloaders' magazines do. The 950 has not seen much professional use, mainly due to its bulk. A submachine gun variant, the Model 960A, also exists, using the same magazine and action with a folding stock and longer barrel.

Caliber: 9mm

Damage: 4

Range: 20 (40 for 960A)

Rate: 4 (21 for 960A)

Clip: 50+1 or 100+1

Conceal: T

Glock 17, 20, 21 and 22: When the Glock 17 debuted on the market in the early 1980s, a sudden media flap occurred concerning its supposed "undetectability." Although the frames of Glock pistols are made of plastics and polymers, the barrels and other internal parts are more than sufficient to show up on X-ray machines and metal detectors. (Additionally, Glock manufactures these pistols with strips of metal in the handle so they *are* visible to detectors.) Perhaps because of their incredible media exposure, Glocks are extremely popular today. Glock manufactures several different models, all of which are listed here for simplicity's sake. Each model listed also has a compact companion model with a 10-round clip (an additional round may still be held in the chamber) and a Conceal of P.

Caliber: 9mm (model 17); .40 S&W (model 22); 10mm (model 20); .45 ACP (model 21)

Damage: 4 for model 17, 5 for all others

Range: 20 for model 17, 25 for all others

Rate: 4 for models 17 and 22, 3 for models 20 and 21

Clip: 17+1 (model 17), 15+1 (models 20 and 22), 13+1 (model 21)

Conceal: J

Heckler & Koch P7M13: The German firm of Heckler & Koch designed this pistol specifically for law enforcement use, combining maximum carrying safety with minimal difficulty in quick-draw and use. The P7M13's safety is part of the grip; it will fire as long as it is held, but the safety automatically engages if hand pressure is released from it, keeping the gun from going off if dropped. All Heckler & Koch weapons have excellent reputations for reliability (and high price), and the P7M13 is no exception.

> **Caliber:** 9mm
> **Damage:** 4
> **Range:** 20
> **Rate:** 4
> **Clip:** 13
> **Conceal:** P

Colt M1911A1: The classic ".45 automatic," the Colt M1911A1 was the standard service sidearm of the U.S. Army from its introduction in 1911 until the mid-1980s. It is still popular in military, law enforcement and civilian applications alike, and is possibly the most widely used pistol in the world. The M1911A1 has been seen in countless films, most recently and vividly in *Last Man Standing*. Lara Croft also uses these in *Tomb Raider*, so they must still be good.

> **Caliber:** .45 ACP (Automatic Colt Pistol)
> **Damage:** 5
> **Range:** 25
> **Rate:** 3
> **Clip:** 7+1 to 9+1, depending on the exact model
> **Conceal:** J

SIG-Sauer P220 and P230: The partnership of Swiss SIG and German J.P. Sauer & Sohn has a reputation for consistently producing excellent weapons. SIG-Sauer offers a number of models of automatic pistols; the two listed here are fairly representative. Special Agents Fox Mulder and Dana Scully of *X-Files* fame carry a P220 and P230, respectively.

> **Caliber:** .45 ACP (P220), .380 (P230)
> **Damage:** 5 (P220), 4 (P230)
> **Range:** 25 (P220), 20 (P230)
> **Rate:** 3
> **Clip:** 7+1
> **Conceal:** J

IMI Desert Eagle: Although many professionals feel that the Desert Eagle is too much gun and too prone to mechanical failure, there is no denying the sheer intimidation factor this weapon carries. The Israeli-made Desert Eagle is the largest, most powerful autoloader in production today, and is almost impossible to fire one-handed (minimum Strength 4). In addition to its most impressive caliber, the Desert Eagle is also available in .357 Magnum and .44 Magnum.

> **Caliber:** .50 Action Express
> **Damage:** 7
> **Range:** 30
> **Rate:** 1
> **Clip:** 7
> **Conceal:** J

Submachine Guns and Machine Pistols

Submachine guns, or SMGs, are designed to bridge the gap between pistols and automatic rifles. They are small weapons (under 3 feet long) that fire pistol-caliber ammunition at a high cyclic rate. Despite their similarity in use and appearance to rifles, SMGs operate internally more like pistols. SMGs are most commonly used by military special operations units, police SWAT teams and gangs, because the relatively close ranges at which all three groups usually enter conflict do not require the use of rifles.

Like automatic pistols, SMGs and machine pistols may hold an additional bullet in the chamber, hence the +1 notation to the Clip Trait. For the most part, chambering this additional round is excessive and time consuming, given the minimal benefit, but some gunbunnies are insistent upon doing it.

Beretta Model 93R: Classified as a machine pistol (a pistol-scale weapon that fires at SMG speeds), the Beretta Model 93R is a three-round-burst-capable version of the Model 92 (above). It incorporates a fold-down forward grip and folding stock. The Model 93R is not capable of true fully automatic fire, which makes it slightly more controllable than other machine pistols.

> **Caliber:** 9mm
> **Damage:** 4
> **Range:** 20
> **Rate:** 15
> **Clip:** 20+1
> **Conceal:** J

Ceska Model 61: More commonly known as the Skorpion, the Czech-made Model 61 is one of the smallest SMGs in production. It was widely used in Soviet bloc militaries, and has found its way into the armories of Third-World nations, terrorist groups and street gangs across the world. The Skorpion's relatively low-powered ammunition and uncontrollability are balanced by its small size and low cost.

> **Caliber:** .32 ACP
> **Damage:** 3
> **Range:** 20
> **Rate:** 15*
> **Clip:** 10+1 or 20+1
> **Conceal:** J

Glock 18: The Glock 18 is a fully automatic machine pistol version of the Glock 17, intended for law enforcement, military and antiterrorist use. Although it is similar in appearance to the Glock 17, it is deliberately designed to have incompatible parts.

Caliber: 9mm
Damage: 4
Range: 20
Rate: 19*
Clip: 17+1, 19+1, or 33+1
Conceal: J

Heckler & Koch MP5 series: The MP5 series is the most well-respected and reliable series of submachineguns in existence. A wide variety of variants exist, including the MP5K, a highly concealable, short-barreled version, and the MP5SD series, whose built-in sound suppresser makes it the quietest SMG in the world (not to mention impossible for civilians to acquire). MP5s can be seen in *Navy SEALs, Die Hard I & II,* and a plethora of other movies. Most Western military special operations units use MP5s.

Caliber: 9mm, though 10mm versions exist
Damage: 4 (5 for 10mm)
Range: 40 (25 for MP5K)
Rate: 21*
Clip: 15+1 or 30+1
Conceal: T (J for MP5K)

IMI Uzi: The Uzi was the first SMG to achieve widespread popularity (or notoriety…). Manufactured in Israel, it has spread across the world. In America, the Uzi is used by the Secret Service and many major police forces. Two smaller variants, the Mini-Uzi and the Micro-Uzi, are identical in function but lack the range and controllability of the larger model.

Caliber: 9mm and .45 ACP (all three models are available in both calibers)
Damage: 4 for 9mm, 5 for .45 ACP
Range: 50 for Uzi, 25 for Mini-Uzi, 15 for Micro-Uzi
Rate: 21*
Clip: 16+1, 20+1, or 32+1 for all models in 9mm; 16 for all models in .45 ACP
Conceal: T (J for Micro-Uzi)

Ingram M10: Also known as the MAC-10, this weapon was introduced in the 1970s and is still renowned for its durability. Its major drawback is its lack of control when firing long bursts, as its trigger allows it to fire *only* full-auto. Practice is required to pull off three-round bursts, and single shots are hard for all but the most skilled operators. A sound suppresser is available, but these are hard to obtain legally.

Caliber: 9mm and .45 ACP
Damage: 4 for 9mm, 5 for .45 ACP
Range: 25
Rate: 32+*
Clip: 32+1
Conceal: J

Intratec TEC-9: Although marketed as a pistol, this weapon is easy to convert to full automatic (Professional Skill: Gunsmith 1 and a decent toolkit gets the job done in an hour or two). Thus, it is encountered quite often in the hands of boneheaded thugs and gangstaz who want something cheap they can spray a room or an alley with. Professionals tend to stick with something less likely to blow up in their hands, as the TEC-9 is made poorly to begin with and impromptu modifications serve only to make it less reliable.

>   **Caliber:** 9mm
>   **Damage:** 4
>   **Range:** 20
>   **Rate:** 18*
>   **Clip:** 20+1 or 32+1
>   **Conceal:** J

Thompson M1928: The once-ubiquitous "Tommy gun" was the first submachine gun used by the U.S. military. Although obsolete today, it is still effective, and was a staple of 1930s gangster films. Its huge optional drum magazine gives it an unmistakable silhouette. Like the MAC-10, its trigger allows it to fire *only* full-auto, making three-round bursts a matter of experience and control.

>   **Caliber:** .45 ACP
>   **Damage:** 5
>   **Range:** 50
>   **Rate:** 15*
>   **Clip:** 20 or 100
>   **Conceal:** T

RIFLES

For game purposes, the category of "rifles" encompasses any gun that is not fully automatic and fires a fast (compared to a pistol round), narrow-diameter bullet down a rifled barrel. Rifles are used for both hunting and sniping; the only difference between the two is often the level of craftsmanship of the weapon. Rifles may be *bolt-action* or *lever-action*, in which cases each shot must be moved into firing position by the user, or *semiautomatic*, where some of the gas or recoil from the previous shot works the action and loads the next round. Most bolt-action rifles feed from internal ammunition supplies rather than snap-in magazines, so they are slower to reload than semiautomatic weapons.

Rifles, like automatic pistols, may chamber a round in addition to those carried in their clip, so they bear the +1 notation to their Clip Trait. This is rarely ever used in practice, however — if you're shooting at something (or someone…) that needs to be hit 31 times to bring it down, maybe you'd better just leave it alone.

Remington Model 700: This is a fairly common bolt-action hunting rifle and a good representative of its type; a variety of other brands have similar Traits, varying only in superficial appearance. The military version of this, the M24 Sniper Weapon System, is modified heavily at the factory and is extremely difficult to acquire (Resources 4, military Allies or Contacts, and a lenient Storyteller).

>   **Caliber:** .30-06 and .308 Remington for Model 700, .300 Winchester Magnum for M24
>   **Damage:** 8 for Model 700, 9 for M24
>   **Range:** 300 for Model 700, 500 for M24
>   **Rate:** 1
>   **Clip:** 5+1, held internally rather than magazine-fed
>   **Conceal:** N

Remington Model 740: This is a smaller-caliber version of the Model 700, and is also a representative sample of its type and caliber.

>   **Caliber:** .223 Remington for civilian versions, 5.56mm for military versions (interchangeable)
>   **Damage:** 7
>   **Range:** 275
>   **Rate:** 3
>   **Clip:** 5+1, held internally
>   **Conceal:** T

Ruger 10/22: Another representative sample of small-caliber rifles used for small game or "plinking," this particular model is semiautomatic, but varieties exist with all forms of actions. It is possible to convert this weapon into a fully automatic (and fully illegal) version with a decent metal shop and the right knowledge (Professional Skill: Gunsmith 2).

>   **Caliber:** .22 LR (Long Rifle)
>   **Damage:** 4
>   **Range:** 100
>   **Rate:** 4
>   **Clip:** 10+1 or 50+1
>   **Conceal:** N

Weatherby Mark V: This is a British-made bolt-action rifle designed for hunting large game such as elephants, rhinos and light aircraft. Its recoil is powerful enough to inflict (7 - character's Strength) dice of Bashing damage on anyone who fires it without being properly braced (Storyteller's discretion: any position where the character is off-balance, firing from the hip, or firing while moving).

>   **Caliber:** .460 Weatherby Magnum
>   **Damage:** 10
>   **Range:** 300+
>   **Rate:** 1
>   **Clip:** 3+1
>   **Conceal:** N

Barrett Model 82 "Light Fifty": The heaviest weapon available on the civilian market, this monstrous 4'9"-long, 35-pound semiautomatic rifle fires the same ammunition used by heavy machine guns. Its hunting applications are dubious at best, though it can be legally owned by private citizens in the United States and most large gun stores can theoretically acquire one. The rifle is known in military service as the M82A1, and is used by U.S. Army Special Forces snipers. The M82A1 was the rifle used by God in

Navy SEALs and by Robocop in *Robocop II*. As with the Weatherby Mark V, the Model 82's recoil can break the shoulder, upper arm, collarbone and/or ribs of an unprepared or weak operator.

    Caliber: .50 BMG (Browning Machine Gun)

    Damage: 12; the .50 BMG round has the combination of velocity and mass to completely ignore any armor or cover lighter than a cinder-block wall or a military vehicle, though Fortitude will still help soak normally.

    Range: Effectively 300, though professional military snipers have claimed kills at over 1500 yards in open terrain

    Rate: 1

    Clip: 11

    Conceal: N

ASSAULT RIFLES

Although semiautomatic versions of most of these weapons do exist, assault rifles are military weapons. They are not generally found in the hands of civilians. For game purposes, this category includes both true *assault rifles*, which fire small rounds at a high rate of fire, and *battle rifles*, which use larger ammunition and fire more slowly. Both are employed in the same roles and can kill a target equally dead.

It should be repeated that weapons with full-auto capability, or even three-round burst capability, are highly illegal for anyone but police and military personnel to use or own. It is possible to acquire semiautomatic collector's versions of these weapons, which can be converted to full-auto by a character with Professional Skill: Gunsmith of 2 or better. However, any use of such weapons will likely draw police and federal attention (the ATF takes a very dim view of such antics). Storytellers should feel free to drop FBI, SWAT and whatever other acronyms they need on their player characters' heads.

    Colt M16: The standard assault rifle of the United States' armed services, among others, the M16's design has been copied for both military and civilian versions. Newer versions are capable of only single shots and three-round bursts, though plenty of older models with true full-automatic capability are still out there. A cut-down carbine version, the M4, features a folding stock and shorter barrel, trading range for size.

    Caliber: 5.56mm

    Damage: 7

    Range: 200 (120 for carbines)

    Rate: 15 or 20, depending on the precise model

    Clip: 20+1 or 30+1

    Conceal: N (T for carbines)

Russian State Arsenals AK-74: The grandchild of the venerable AK-47, the AK-74 was the standard Soviet bloc assault rifle before the collapse of the USSR, and hasn't gone out of style. A variety of versions are out there; the only ones that really matter to game play are the folding-stocked variants and carbines.

> **Caliber:** 5.45mm
> **Damage:** 7
> **Range:** 200 (120 for carbines)
> **Rate:** 20
> **Clip:** 30
> **Conceal:** N (T for carbines)

Steyr AUG: The Austrian-made AUG (Armee Universal Gewehr) is surprising in that such a unique weapon has actually been adopted by multiple militaries. The AUG is a bullpup-configuration weapon, which means that its magazine and action are placed in the stock, behind the grip and trigger. This allows a shorter overall design with no loss of barrel length. The AUG also mounts an integral telescopic scope (see below) in its carrying handle. However, its most revolutionary feature is its modular construction: one AUG and a few conversion parts can be broken down and reassembled into a light machine gun, a submachine gun, a short carbine or the basic assault rifle configuration in about 15 minutes.

> **Caliber:** 5.56mm (9mm in SMG configuration)
> **Damage:** 7 (4 in SMG configuration)
> **Range:** 200 (50 for SMG configuration)
> **Rate:** 21
> **Clip:** 42+1 (30+1 in SMG configuration)
> **Conceal:** T (N for light machinegun configuration)

Colt M14, FN FAL, and Heckler & Koch G3: These 1950s-vintage battle rifles all saw — and still see — widespread use outside their countries of origin. The American M14 (in semiautomatic forms) is found in civilian hands and in Southeast Asia, the Belgian FAL is common in Africa, and the German G3 sees heavy use in South America. All three weapons have effectively equal game statistics; the G3 is about a pound heavier and probably more reliable than the other two, if anyone's checking. A version of the M14, the M21, is still in use in the U.S. Army as a sniper's rifle.

> **Caliber:** 7.62mm
> **Damage:** 8
> **Range:** 275
> **Rate:** 10
> **Clip:** 20+1
> **Conceal:** N

Russian State Arsenals AK-47: The AK-47 is probably the most widely distributed battle rifle in the world. Although its ammunition has been criticized as being low-powered and unstable at long ranges, the Soviets didn't seem to complain. The AK-47 has a reputation for reliability

under the worst field conditions. As with the AK-74, there are folding-stock variants which can be hidden under long coats with a little practice.

> **Caliber:** 7.62mm Soviet, not interchangeable with other 7.62mm ammunition
> **Damage:** 8
> **Range:** 250
> **Rate:** 10
> **Clip:** 30+1
> **Conceal:** N (T for folding stock)

SHOTGUNS

Shotguns are large-bore weapons (typically about half an inch) that fire either slugs or clusters of pellets down a smooth barrel. Shotguns are limited in range and ammunition capacity, bulky and punishing in their recoil, but they are intimidating as all hell and viciously destructive in close quarters. Shotguns are pump-, lever- or slide-action or semiautomatic. There are a few fully automatic shotguns available; these resemble large assault rifles and are nigh impossible to control and highly illegal to own. Unless otherwise noted, all of these shotguns feed from internal ammunition supplies (which makes them slower to reload than magazine-fed weapons).

Generic double-barreled hunting shotgun: Double-barreled shotguns are perhaps the ultimate in simple firearms. A wide assortment is available on the open market. Double-barreled shotguns can be cut down and sawed off for concealment at the expense of range and legality (and the risk of breaking the shooter's wrist without a stock with which to brace against the recoil).

> **Caliber:** 12-gauge
> **Damage:** 8
> **Range:** 20, 10, or 5, depending on barrel length
> **Rate:** 2; both barrels can be fired as a single action, using the same roll to hit for both rounds
> **Clip:** 2
> **Conceal:** N normally, but cut-down versions can reach T or even J

Benelli M3 Super 90: This is a semi-automatic shotgun in widespread use among SWAT teams, and a fairly representative example of its type.

> **Caliber:** 12-gauge
> **Damage:** 8
> **Range:** 20
> **Rate:** 3
> **Clip:** 7
> **Conceal:** T

Remington 870P, Ithaca M37, and Mossberg M500: These three pump-action shotguns are all in widespread use by regular police forces. In other words, one of these is what the cops are likely to pull out of the cruiser when responding to the disturbance your characters are causing. All of these can be cut down for concealment at the expense of effective range.

Caliber: 12-gauge

Damage: 8

Range: 20 (10 for cut-down versions)

Rate: 1

Clip: 5 (8 for Remington 870P)

Conceal: N (T for cut-down versions)

Franchi SPAS-12: This futuristic-looking semiautomatic shotgun is also in wide use by police forces across North America and Europe. It can be switched into pump-action mode (Rate drops to 1) in case of a malfunction. Its folding stock has a highly unusual brace that swings out to allow the weapon to be fired with one hand if it's still in semi-auto mode. This is the weapon Sarah Connor had at the end of *Terminator 2*.

Caliber: 12-gauge

Damage: 8

Range: 20

Rate: 3

Clip: 7

Conceal: N

Daewoo USAS-12: A highly unusual (and vicious) weapon from South Korea, this beast is a military shotgun with fully automatic capability. It is designed to look and operate like an oversized assault rifle, though its recoil is punishing at best and splinters ribs at worst. Malfunctions and mistakes with this weapon tend to be… spectacular.

Caliber: 12-gauge

Damage: 8

Range: 20

Rate: 6

Clip: 12 (magazine) or 28 (drum)

Conceal: N

FIREARM ACCESSORIES

Telescopic Scopes: The most common variety of scope is the telescopic one, which magnifies the image of the target to enhance a weapon's effective range when aiming. Scopes add two dice to the character's dice pool score when making an aimed shot. This bonus applies after one turn of aiming and is cumulative with the Perception bonus for aim. An aimed shot made with the aid of a scope also increases the distance for a "medium-range" shot's distance by 50 percent (increase the weapon's Range Trait by 50 percent). A scope may be mounted on any rifle or assault rifle, and some revolvers or bolt-action pistols may mount scopes as well (see individual weapon listings above). Automatic pistols may not mount scopes, as this would interfere with the weapon's operation.

Installing a scope of any type requires Firearms 3 (or Professional Skill: Gunsmith 1), one hour, and 20 rounds of ammunition (which are used to ensure that the scope is aligned properly). Scopes that are improperly installed, or are knocked out of alignment, provide no bonus of any sort.

Night-Vision Scopes: Surplus night-vision equipment is becoming more and more common on the open market, though it is still quite expensive. Night-vision gear comes in three forms: light amplification (starlight), infrared (IR), and thermal.

Starlight equipment amplifies available visible light to a level approximating daylight. It does not function in total darkness. Starlight scopes reduce the difficulty modifiers for darkness by one, but will not reduce them below +1. Starlight scopes require a minimum Resources 2 to acquire.

IR gear converts invisible infrared light to a visible black-and-white image. Like starlight equipment, IR scopes and goggles do not function in total darkness. However, infrared equipment can benefit from an infrared flashlight or spotlight, which is invisible to the unaided eye. IR gear is available in both scope and goggle forms. IR equipment reduces the difficulty modifiers for darkness by two, but will not reduce them below +1. IR gear requires a minimum Resources 3 to purchase.

Thermal vision equipment is more sophisticated than starlight or IR, and literally displays heat as an electronic image. Thermal sights "see" through smoke or fog and can find living targets through thin walls. They do not pick up a vampire as more than a blurred image, however, unless the vampire has fed within the past two hours. Thermal vision equipment reduces the difficulty modifiers for darkness, fog or smoke by up to three and cover by one. Precipitation, however, reduces thermal vision gear's effectiveness (difficulties for darkness are only reduced by one and cover applies normally). Thermal scopes are primarily military equipment and require Resources 4 to purchase. They are legal, but government officials may make discreet inquiries about anyone who buys a thermal scope.

Laser Sights: Modern laser sights are negligible in weight. They attach to any weapon, but are most commonly used on pistols or SMGs. A laser sight projects a thin, very low-powered beam of light, typically red, which appears as a small dot on the target at which the gun is aimed. This is not enough to blind the human eye, though temporary dazzling may result (Storyteller's discretion for effects). Laser sights are widely available to anyone with the funds (Resources 3). The game effect of a laser sight is to add one die to the dice pool of any aimed shot made at a range of 30 yards or less.

Silencers and Suppressers: "Silencer" is often a misnomer, as very few firearms are totally silent. Guns make noise in three ways: the explosion of the round firing, the crack of the bullet breaking the sound barrier, and the metal against metal noise of the gun's action. To truly silence a gun, one must eliminate all three of these noise sources.

Most sound-suppressed weapons reduce noise by venting the exhaust gases from the round through a series of baffles that slow the gas to subsonic speeds (slowing the bullet in the process, as the expanding gas that propels it bleeds away). As pistol-caliber ammunition typically is slower than rifle ammunition and relies on mass over speed to cause damage, pistols and SMGs are easier to suppress than rifles. Any silencer strong enough to be effective on a rifle slows the bullet enough to reduce the weapon's Damage Trait by 2 or more, and some rounds (such as shotgun rounds or the .50-caliber BMG bullet) are too large to silence at all.

Silencers are bulky, often as long as the gun itself. Any weapon that has a silencer fitted to it rises one level in its Conceal Trait (e.g. a pistol with Conceal P goes to Conceal J when a silencer is attached).

The larger the round, the more difficult it is to suppress it. Generally, any gun with a Damage Trait higher than 4 cannot truly be silenced, only suppressed. For example, a suppressed Colt M1911A1 (firing .45 caliber ammunition, Damage 5) is about as loud as a dictionary being slammed on a table. While obvious as a loud noise, this may not be immediately recognizable as a gunshot.

Silencers are highly illegal for civilians to own without proper government permits, and quite difficult to acquire. A very skilled gunsmith might be able to build one from scratch if given tools and time (Professional Skill: Gunsmith of at least 4 and a minimum of one week), but its reliability would be questionable.

Disguised Weapons: It is possible to build a weapon, typically a submachine gun, into a briefcase or a similarly unobtrusive object (with Professional Skill: Gunsmith 4). The most common configuration is to place the weapon entirely inside the container with a blow-away patch over the muzzle and a mechanical linkage to the trigger to allow the character to fire the weapon without opening whatever it is hidden within. This allows the gun to be fired (at a +2 difficulty, and no aimed shots are possible). A weapon firing in this fashion is immediately obvious due to the muzzle flash, even if it is silenced. The container must be opened in order to reload the weapon.

The Heckler & Koch MP5K, the Glock 19 and the Ingram M10 can all be acquired with briefcases or satchels designed for the weapon in question. In most cases, there is a trigger assembly built into the briefcase's carrying handle, and the gun may be removed and used normally should the situation require such action.

Melee Weapons

Melee Weapon Traits

Damage: The base number of damage dice rolled after a successful strike. For melee weapons, this is based on the character's Strength Trait (and Potence, if any) plus a number of dice determined by the size, mass and design of the weapon in question.

Conceal: The amount of clothing under which the weapon may be hidden. P = in a pocket, J = under a jacket, T = under a trench coat, and N = the weapon is too large to carry concealed.

Minimum Strength: The minimum Strength (Potence applies to this total) that a character must have in order to wield the weapon in combat.

Blunt Weapons

Blunt weapons do bashing damage unless otherwise noted or a called strike to the head is used.

Small Clubs: This category includes blackjacks, quarter rolls stuffed into socks, collapsible tactical batons, tonfas, jo staves and lengths of lead pipe. Anything that is used to bash rather than slash and is less than around two feet in length is considered a small club for game purposes.

> **Damage:** Strength +1 (add or subtract a die if the weapon in question is particularly heavy or light)
>
> **Conceal:** J (P for collapsible batons or blackjacks)
>
> **Minimum Strength:** 1

Large Clubs: Anything longer than two feet but shorter than about four and a half is considered a large club. This includes canes, baseball bats, pool cues, cavalry maces and staves that have been broken in half by angry Brujah.

> **Damage:** Strength +2 (add a die or two for exceptionally heavy weapons such as maces or bats; subtract one for flimsy, improvised ones)
>
> **Conceal:** T
>
> **Minimum Strength:** 2

Staves: Staves are generally defined as "as tall as the wielder and as thick around as her fist," but any long blunt implement that's too large to be used with one hand is a staff for game purposes.

> **Damage:** Strength +3, with a definite reach advantage
>
> **Conceal:** N
>
> **Minimum Strength:** 1

Edged Weapons

Edged weapons do lethal damage unless otherwise indicated.

Knives: This category encompasses everything from steak knives to Bowie knives to Japanese

tantos. The line between "knife" and "short sword" is generally drawn at about 12 inches. Fighting knives, which are generally double edged and balanced for the express purpose of rapid strikes in melee combat, tend to be illegal in many areas.

> **Damage:** Strength +1
> **Conceal:** P or J, depending on size and style
> **Minimum Strength:** 1

Foils and rapiers: Lightweight swords used primarily for sport fencing in the modern era, most rapiers have no edge and a blunted tip. However, it's not that hard to sharpen one, and many Ventrue elders remember a time when gentlemen wore rapiers as a matter of fashion. Rapiers and foils are used to stab and thrust rather than slash, and will not parry heavier weapons without the risk of breakage (Storyteller's discretion).

> **Damage:** Strength +2 (bashing, unless the tip is sharpened)
> **Conceal:** T
> **Minimum Strength:** 1

Sabers, katanas and scimitars: Sabers and scimitars tend to have curved blades between two and three feet in length. Sabers are European in origin, katanas are Japanese, and scimitars come from the Middle East.

> **Damage:** Strength +2
> **Conceal:** T
> **Minimum Strength:** 2

Broadswords and longswords: These are generally thought of as European weapons, although the idea has come up in every civilization at some point or another. They are usually three feet or so long with straight, heavy blades.

> **Damage:** Strength +3
> **Conceal:** T
> **Minimum Strength:** 2

Two-handed swords: Just what the name implies, these massive implements of personal injury are between four and six feet long and require both hands to use effectively (Strength + Potence of at least 7 is needed to swing one with one hand, as the balance is as much a factor as the weight).

> **Damage:** Strength +5
> **Conceal:** N
> **Minimum Strength:** 4

Miscellaneous Weapons

Brass knuckles and sap gloves: These are designed to increase the force of hand strikes. Punches from a character wearing brass knuckles or sap gloves (gloves with pockets of lead shot sewn into the knuckles) do an additional die of bashing damage. Characters making attacks with claws do not gain this benefit.

Whips and chains: Aside from the recreational uses, some people swear by the versatility of a flexible weapon. Whips can be used to slash, or can entangle (treat as a grapple attack at range). Chains aren't quite as useful in that role, but hit harder.

> **Damage:** Strength +1 (+2 for chains)
> **Conceal:** J
> **Minimum Strength:** 1

THROWN WEAPONS

See Chapter Six of **Vampire: The Masquerade** for the basic rules for throwing. Thrown weapons cause lethal damage unless otherwise noted. They use the same Traits as melee weapons.

Darts and shuriken: Darts and shuriken (throwing stars) are usually too small to do much damage in and of themselves, but they can easily be coated with various chemical compounds.

> **Damage:** Strength -1
> **Conceal:** P
> **Minimum Strength:** 1

Knives and hatchets: Most knives and hatchets are far from aerodynamic; those that are balanced for throwing aren't always the best choice for hand-to-hand combat and *vice versa* (+2 to difficulties if using one type of weapon for the opposite application). It is possible to throw a knife or hatchet so that the hilt strikes the target instead of the blade, thus inflicting bashing damage rather than lethal (+1 difficulty to hit, and requires Throwing 1).

> **Damage:** Strength +1
> **Conceal:** P or J
> **Minimum Strength:** 1

Spears: Although spears are rather uncommon in the modern world, they are sometimes still an effective recourse, particularly if the thrower is skilled enough to aim for the heart. Some ancient cultures used spear-throwers, or *atlatls*, which are little more than four- to six-foot sticks with notches at one end to hold the spear. An *atlatl* functions as a lever, giving the thrower two more points of Strength for the purpose of determining range, difficulty and damage.

> **Damage:** Strength +2
> **Conceal:** N
> **Minimum Strength:** 2

ARCHERY

Bows cause lethal damage by cutting and slashing rather than by impact, as arrows travel too slowly to cause much in the way of hydrostatic shock (the primary source of damage from bullets). This allows bows to penetrate most modern body armor, which is

designed to defend against bullets, with relative ease (half the normal soak bonus, rounded down). They use the same Traits as melee weapons, with the addition of the Range Trait of firearms.

Characters using bows may take aim as per the aimed shot rules for firearms. It takes one action to fire a bow and one action to reload; reloading can be accomplished in the same turn as firing with two successes on a Dexterity + Archery roll (difficulty 7).

Unlike bullets, arrows can be made without special shop tools. Any character with Archery 3 and access to appropriate materials (stone or metal arrowheads, feathers, wood for shafts, glue, string and a knife) may construct arrows at a rate of one per hour.

Short Bow: This encompasses all bows that are between three and four feet long. Short bows may be fired from horseback. Anyone with Archery 3 or higher and a week to work can make a short bow.

> **Damage:** 2
> **Conceal:** T
> **Minimum Strength:** 2
> **Range:** 60

Long Bow: This includes such weapons as the Welsh longbow, which ended the military dominance of the armored European knight, and the Japanese *daikyu*, a seven-foot-tall cavalry bow. Long bows may be designed to be fired on foot or fired while mounted on a horse, but not both. A character with Archery 4 or higher and 10 days of working time can make her own long bow.

> **Damage:** 4
> **Conceal:** N
> **Minimum Strength:** 4
> **Range:** 120

Small Compound Bow: Compound bows use a system of pulleys to enhance the user's strength, thus allowing the same amount of power to be delivered with less effort. Compound bows are a relatively new innovation, and may not be constructed without specific tools. A small compound bow is about three feet long.

> **Damage:** 2
> **Conceal:** N
> **Minimum Strength:** 1
> **Range:** 90

Large Compound Bow: Large compound bows are the most commonly used hunting and target shooting bows. They are typically four feet long or larger.

> **Damage:** 3
> **Conceal:** N
> **Minimum Strength:** 2
> **Range:** 120

Crossbow: A crossbow is a mechanical device that vaguely resembles a modern rifle. It consists of a horizontal bow attached to the front end of a stock. The bow is drawn by crank or by hand, and the projectile (called a bolt or a quarrel) is placed in the stock. A mechanical trigger holds the bow drawn until it is ready to be fired. A crossbow takes five actions to re-draw and reload.

> **Damage:** 5
> **Conceal:** T
> **Minimum Strength:** 2
> **Range:** 20

Personal Armor

The modern media has perpetuated the perception that a "bulletproof vest" will stop anything that hits it, leaving the wearer little more than stunned. Sadly, this is not the case. Currently produced body armor is designed to absorb and spread the force of a high-velocity impact. The full amount of kinetic energy delivered by a bullet still hits the wearer — it's just spread over the entire area of the armor before it's transferred to the tender flesh and bone of the body. This usually results in spectacular bruising over the entire torso, a few cracked ribs and a few minutes of disorientation and panic.

Furthermore, body armor is only fully effective against relatively low-velocity rounds (pistol ammunition, in other words). Bullets with higher velocities (rifle rounds) typically punch right through such synthetic fibers as Kevlar and Spectra. On the other hand, melee weapons such as knives or clubs treat body armor like any other thick clothing, and cut or smash the wearer right through the material.

Some Kindred elders still keep metal armor from centuries past. This is both more obvious and less bullet-resistant than modern body armor, but it generally stops melee and brawling attacks more effectively than its present-night counterpart.

Unless otherwise noted, the armor listed below covers only the wearer's torso and thus does not protect against fire, sunlight, called shots to the head, neck, or limbs, or explosions.

Body armor is expensive. Unless otherwise noted in the entry below, assume that a character must have a minimum Resources of 3 to purchase modern armor and Resources 4 to purchase archaic armor (cheaper reproductions are available, but these are meant for display rather than use). Body armor is also rarely "one size fits all", and poorly fitted (read: stolen) body armor may have an increased Dexterity penalty at the Storyteller's discretion.

It bears mention that the armor Traits presented here are a bit more complex than those presented on page 214 of **Vampire: The Masquerade**. Storytellers who wish to keep complexity to a minimum should feel free to use those Traits instead.

Armor Traits

Bashing Soak: The number of dice that the armor adds to the wearer's soak dice pool against bashing damage. This is also the value used against thrown weapons.

Melee Soak: The number of dice that the armor adds to the wearer's soak dice pool against lethal damage from melee weapons. This is also the value used against lethal brawling attacks (e.g. Feral Claws) and low-velocity projectiles such as arrows or crossbow bolts.

Bullet Soak: The number of dice that the armor adds to the wearer's soak dice pool against lethal damage from guns.

Dexterity Penalty: The amount by which the wearer's Dexterity is reduced while wearing the armor. This may not reduce the Attribute below 1.

Perception Penalty: The amount by which the wearer's Perception is reduced while wearing the item. This may not reduce the Attribute below 1. This Trait applies only to helmets.

Conceal: The amount of clothing under which the armor may be hidden. W = windbreaker or loose shirt, J = jacket or suit, T = trench coat, N = the armor is too bulky to wear concealed.

Modern Armor

Reinforced clothing: This is less of a formal category of body armor than it is a mode of dress. "Reinforced clothing" covers such garb as biker's leathers or the heavy insulated jumpsuits worn by hunters and construction crews.

> **Bashing Soak:** 2
> **Melee Soak:** 1
> **Bullet Soak:** 0
> **Dexterity Penalty:** 0
> **Conceal:** N/A, as these are normal clothes

Armor T-shirt: This is a thin Kevlar garment worn under street clothing, typically a loose shirt or sweater. It provides minimal protection, but is easy to wear concealed.

> **Bashing Soak:** 2
> **Melee Soak:** 0
> **Bullet Soak:** 1
> **Dexterity Penalty:** 0
> **Conceal:** W

Light Ballistic Vest: This is a vest designed to be worn under a loose shirt or sweater as the armor T-shirt. Because it is thicker but designed for the same ease of concealment, it impairs movement more than does the shirt.

> **Bashing Soak:** 2
> **Melee Soak:** 1
> **Bullet Soak:** 2
> **Dexterity Penalty:** 1
> **Conceal:** W

Medium Ballistic Vest: The most common type of body armor worn by security guards and uniformed police officers, this is designed to be worn over or under clothes, depending on the

ANDREW TRABBOLD '98

situation in which the wearer expects to find herself. This type of body armor comes with inside pockets where ceramic or metal "trauma plates" can be inserted for extra protection. Some models are designed expressly for combat wear and incorporate a variety of pockets for radios, spare magazines and other tools of the trade.

Bashing Soak: 2 (3 with trauma plates)

Melee Soak: 1 (3 with trauma plates)

Bullet Soak: 3 (4 with trauma plates)

Dexterity Penalty: 1 (2 with trauma plates)

Conceal: J

Flak Jacket: This is usually the same approximate thickness as a medium ballistic vest, but it extends to cover the arms and, sometimes, the lower abdomen. Flak jackets also provide minimal (one die of soak) protection against explosions.

Bashing Soak: 3

Melee Soak: 2

Bullet Soak: 4

Dexterity Penalty: 2

Conceal: T

SWAT Tactical Jacket: Made primarily for SWAT and hostage rescue teams, these garments are very expensive (minimum Resources 5 for civilians to purchase) and tend to draw police scrutiny if seen on civilians. SWAT jackets are designed for maximum ballistic protection with a minimum impact on mobility. They are designed to be worn over clothing (usually including an armor T-shirt) and cover the wearer from the shoulders down to the groin. They usually feature trauma plates and equipment pouches. The Dexterity penalty of a SWAT jacket is reduced to 1 for activities which rely primarily on the hands and arms (such as shooting).

Bashing Soak: 3

Melee Soak: 3

Bullet Soak: 4

Dexterity Penalty: 2

Conceal: T

Riot Gear: Although it's impossible to cover all the bases where personal injury is concerned, riot gear does make the attempt. This usually includes full protection for the torso and partial protection for the arms and legs against both melee and firearm attacks. Like a flak jacket, riot gear provides minimal (one die of soak) protection against explosions.

Bashing Soak: 4

Melee Soak: 4

Bullet Soak: 5

Dexterity Penalty: 3

Conceal: N

Bomb Disposal Suit: Explosions are perhaps the hardest source of combat injury to armor an individual against. Bomb disposal suits are designed specifically to defend against concussion and shrapnel, and add six dice to the wearer's soak dice pool for explosions only. The Dexterity penalty of a bomb disposal suit does not apply to delicate operations (such as defusing a booby trap).

> **Bashing Soak:** 4
> **Melee Soak:** 4
> **Bullet Soak:** 2
> **Dexterity Penalty:** 3
> **Conceal:** N

Nomex Suit: This is a specialized item worn almost exclusively by race car drivers, firefighters and SWAT troopers. Nomex is a very expensive (minimum Resources 4) flame-retardant fabric. A Nomex suit typically covers the entire body except for the hands and head, and comes with gloves and a ski mask to protect those two areas. It provides three additional soak dice for the sole purpose of resisting fire. A Nomex suit is designed to be worn under clothing.

> **Bashing Soak:** 0
> **Melee Soak:** 0
> **Bullet Soak:** 0
> **Dexterity Penalty:** 0
> **Conceal:** W

Tailored Armor: In recent years, several companies have begun re-tailoring Kevlar or similar materials into name-brand clothing. Typically, windbreakers, sweaters, jackets, tuxedos and business suits are modified to order. This process is very expensive (minimum Resources 4) but the result is virtually unidentifiable as body armor — a Perception + Streetwise roll (difficulty 10, dropping to 8 if Style is rolled instead of Streetwise) is necessary to recognize it.

> **Bashing Soak:** 0
> **Melee Soak:** 0
> **Bullet Soak:** 2
> **Dexterity Penalty:** 0
> **Conceal:** see above

ARCHAIC ARMOR

Imagine someone walking down your street in a suit of chainmail. Consider that reaction when taking the concealability of archaic armor into account.

Composite Armor: This usually consists of leather sewn with metal rings and studs, and perhaps some light chain mail. Composite armor covers the torso, arms and upper legs.

> **Bashing Soak:** 2
> **Melee Soak:** 3
> **Bullet Soak:** 0
> **Dexterity Penalty:** 1
> **Conceal:** T

Heavy Armor: This is a suit of ring mail or chain mail worn over a thick layer of quilted padding. Heavy armor, as the name suggests, is quite heavy and a character must have a minimum Strength of 3 to make use of it.

Bashing Soak: 4

Melee Soak: 4

Bullet Soak: 0

Dexterity Penalty: 1

Conceal: N

Full Knight's Armor: Also referred to as "plate mail," this is what is normally thought of as full medieval armor. Actually, armor of this type was only used for a century or so before the Welsh longbow (and, later, the gun) rendered it obsolete. A minimum Resources of 4 is necessary to locate and purchase a suit of this type of armor that will fit the character, and a minimum Strength of 3 is required to wear it.

Bashing Soak: 5

Melee Soak: 6

Bullet Soak: 1 (Note that metal breaches inward — gunshot wounds are likely to be quite painful…)

Dexterity Penalty: 2

Conceal: N

Helmets

Helmets protect the head and, in some cases, the neck. Their soak values do not add to those of the suits of armor above, but are used separately for attacks that specifically target the head. A helmet is not a sure bet — a bullet deflected by one still transmits enough energy to break the wearer's neck. All helmets, obviously, are impossible to conceal when worn.

Military Helmet: Available in army surplus stores for a relatively low price, this is mainly designed to protect against shrapnel rather than bullets or bludgeons.

Bashing Soak: 1

Melee Soak: 1

Bullet Soak: 1

Perception Penalty: 0

SWAT Helmet: This is similar in construction to the military helmet, but is more heavily padded against melee attacks and has a transparent Plexiglas face shield and a padded neck cover. Some models substitute a gas mask for the face shield (increase Perception penalty to 2).

Bashing Soak: 2

Melee Soak: 2

Bullet Soak: 2

Perception Penalty: 1

Light Helm: Typically worn with heavy archaic armor, this is a padded metal helmet that protects the back and sides of the wearer's head.

Bashing Soak: 1

Melee Soak: 2

Bullet Soak: 0

Perception Penalty: 1

Full Helm: This is worn with a full suit of knight's armor. It is extremely heavy and uncomfortable, but it covers the wearer's entire head and neck.

> **Bashing Soak:** 2
> **Melee Soak:** 3
> **Bullet Soak:** 0
> **Perception Penalty:** 2

Explosives

Explosives cause massive property damage at best, and their use may be viewed as a serious breach of the Masquerade due to the intense investigation from federal authorities (any bombing of a public building is a federal crime and will be investigated by the FBI and ATF). Players who believe their characters can "get away with it" are referred to the examples of the Oklahoma City and World Trade Center bombings. More than likely, elder Kindred will *assist* the authorities in such an investigation — no prince likes that sort of thing going on in her city. Almost all explosives are very difficult to acquire or manufacture, and Storytellers should have no qualms whatsoever about arbitrarily denying anything in this section to characters. The nastier something looks, the less likely it is to fall into the hands of those who would misuse it.

However, sometimes the only way to fix the problem is to blow it up, as has been illustrated in innumerable horror films and stories. Anarchs aren't the only ones who take this view: The Inquisition, for instance, is not above drastic measures. Characters may find themselves on the receiving end of any of the following substances.

Body armor generally does not protect against an explosion, although it may protect against the shrapnel thrown by one (see **Personal Armor** above). All explosions do lethal damage unless otherwise indicated, though characters at ground zero may well suffer aggravated damage, at the Storyteller's discretion — if there's a chance of their survival at all.

Grenades

Grenades are manufactured devices containing relatively small amounts of explosives or chemical substances. They are designed to be used by unskilled troops, and thus require no Demolitions roll to use. However, they do require a Throwing or Athletics roll to be thrown to the desired spot. Grenades are extremely difficult for anyone but police and military personnel to acquire.

Fragmentation grenade: The archetypal grenade, these are designed to propel hundreds of metal and wire shards in all directions upon detonation. The shrapnel, rather than the actual explosion, causes most of the damage. Fragmentation grenades do 12 dice of damage at the center of their explosion, reduced by one die for every yard of distance from the blast.

Concussion grenade: Concussion grenades are designed to incapacitate or kill through their explosion. They are theoretically non-lethal, but no explosion is truly "safe." Concussion grenades are the type most likely to be employed by SWAT teams. They do eight dice of damage, reduced by one die per yard of distance from the blast.

Chemical grenades: This category encompasses both smoke and tear gas grenades, which function identically except for their chemical payload. Both emit gas through holes in their cases rather than exploding. However, the chemical reaction that produces the gas also produces heat, and any character who tries to pick one of these up while it is "active" receives two levels of aggravated damage (soakable with Fortitude, difficulty 6). The clouds produced by these grenades fill a 10-yard radius and last for 10 minutes in relatively still air.

White phosphorus grenades: White phosphorus, or WP, grenades, are ostensibly intended for smoke generation. However, they produce their smoke through the burning of a phosphorus compound that cannot be extinguished without special chemicals. WP grenades inflict damage as fragmentation grenades, but WP damage is aggravated and continues to burn, being reduced by two dice each turn until it burns out. Any flammable substance (like vampires) in the radius of effect of a WP grenade maybe ignited at the Storyteller's discretion. WP grenades are extremely difficult to acquire, and Storytellers should feel free to arbitrarily deny them to characters.

Prepared Charges

This category includes any demolition or blasting charge that has been assembled with an explosive, detonator and detonation method (radio control, timer, etc.) when it enters a character's hands. Prepared charges require no special knowledge to use as general-purpose explosives, but a minimum of Demolitions 2 is necessary to set one and use it in its intended role.

Satchel charges: This is a catchall term for a two-pound mass of plastic explosive and a timer in a canvas bag. Satchel charges are designed to be thrown or dropped and fled, as the timers are usually 15 to 30 seconds long. A satchel charge does 20 dice of damage when it goes off, reduced by one die per two yards of distance from the blast.

Frame charges: These are also known as entry charges. They are small amounts of plastic explosive in an adjustable wood or plastic frame, and are designed to be locked into the frames of heavy doors or windows in order to blow them open. The most common use of frame charges is by SWAT teams in situations where rapid entry into a barricaded area is needed. Frame charges can generally open any door short of a bank vault if properly emplaced, and do six dice of damage to bystanders, reduced by two dice per yard of distance.

Shaped charges: This is more of a technique than a specific type of explosive device. Shaped charges are amounts

of explosive material which have been constructed to direct a majority of the explosion's force in a specific direction. The Storyteller is free to decide the precise game effects of a shaped charge, but generally damage will be increased by 50 percent in the direction that the charge is intended to blow and reduced by 50 percent in other directions. Frame charges (above) are a common application of shaped charges. Shaped charges are also used extensively in demolitions work, whereby buildings are "imploded" by the destruction of key structural supports without flinging lethal shrapnel into the surrounding neighborhood.

Explosive Compounds

All Damage Traits listed are per pound of explosive present unless otherwise noted, and reduce by one die per yard of distance from the blast center. Storytellers may feel free to increase this for dramatic purposes — or to make a point to unruly characters.

Black powder: This is perhaps the only explosive that can be easily and legally acquired in any significant amount. Black powder must be packed tightly; it merely burns if scattered. Black powder can be detonated by heat or an open flame.

Damage: 1

Blasting powder: Blasting powder is an enhanced formula of black powder used in commercial mining operations.

Damage: 2

Nitroglycerine: Nitroglycerine is a clear, oily liquid. It is rather powerful, but it is also extremely unstable. In fact, it is likely to spontaneously detonate if subjected to such shocks as a character running with it. Nitroglycerine also detonates if exposed to heat or flame.

Damage: 3

Dynamite: Also known as trinitrotoluene (TNT), dynamite is nitroglycerine stabilized in an absorbing compound and rolled into sticks. Dynamite that is subjected to temperature changes over an extended period of time "sweats" pure, unstable nitroglycerine. Modern mass-produced dynamite can be detonated only with a specialized primer compound and may safely be ignited as an emergency flare.

Damage: 3 per stick

Plastic explosive: Plastic explosive is a generic term used to describe a number of similar compounds, such as American C-4 or Czech Semtex, which are stable and flexible. Plastic explosives will burn without detonating, and can be used to cook on. They can be detonated only by a primer charge such as a blasting cap or det cord. Plastic explosives can be molded like modeling clay and are the explosive of choice for military applications.

Damage: 1 to 20, depending on the precise compound

Primer cord: Also known as det cord or instant fuse, this is a specialized explosive compound manufactured in ropelike spools. Primer cord is used to detonate separate charges simultaneously. It can also be used as a main charge in some situations, such as cutting down trees, by a skilled explosive technician (Demolitions 3+). Primer cord can be detonated by a primer charge or by open flame.

Damage: 1 per two yards

Blasting caps: These are small charges, detonated by electricity or flame, designed to set off other explosives. They can sometimes be detonated by strong magnetic fields (Storyteller's discretion).

Damage: 4 if a character is in contact with a blasting cap when it goes off, but no effect past a foot or so of distance

Napalm: Napalm is gasoline that has been jellied to make it thick and sticky. It can be extinguished by being completely submerged or by oxygen deprivation, but otherwise burns indefinitely (in game terms — five to 10 minutes becomes irrelevant after the first 20 health levels of aggravated damage). Napalm can be ignited by anything that would ignite regular gasoline. If a character is unfortunate enough to be coated with napalm, roll one die. That many dice of aggravated damage (difficulty 7 to soak with Fortitude) are inflicted on the unfortunate soul on the first turn, and the napalm continues to burn, inflicting one less die of damage per turn until it reaches zero.

MILITARY-GRADE WEAPONRY

Military weapons should never fall into the hands of player characters in a **Vampire: The Masquerade** game. Heavy machine guns, tanks, attack helicopters, artillery, jet fighters and the like are so far outside the scope of personal combat as to be completely ludicrous. The modern battlefield is deadlier than can be described to anyone who hasn't been on one, and Kindred, for all their power, are no match for correctly used modern military technology. No reasonable amount of Potence allows a character to slug it out with a tank that mounts a 120mm main gun firing 100-pound armor-piercing sabot rounds. No realistic amount of Celerity makes a character fast enough to outrun an artillery barrage that saturates every inch of ground in a one-mile radius with shrapnel. No obtainable amount of Fortitude gives a character enough extra soak dice to survive the detonation of a 2000-pound laser-guided bomb. The Kindred are mighty personally, but on the modern battlefield, one character's personal might matters very little in the face of combined arms. As for Kindred of great age and potency, none has reportedly ever dealt with weapons matching their own sheer deadliness. The Storyteller is advised to use military force for dramatic effect alone.

Using the Character Sheet

Not everyone needs to use the expanded character sheet, but many players prefer them, keeping all of their characters' details at their fingertips rather than scattered over notebooks, cocktail napkins and thrice-folded scraps of typing paper. In the interests of saving space in future **Vampire** books, this sheet has been generalized here, so everyone gains maximum use from it.

When filling out the character sheet, remember:

• If your character has the Virtue of Conscience and/or Self-Control, you start out with a "free" dot in those Virtues. Only those horrid individuals with Conviction and/or Instinct don't start with the free dot.

• The Other Traits section of the character sheet can cover any numerical Trait you feel like recording. These are most often Secondary Abilities, but some other Traits are too rare to warrant their own section on the character sheet (True Faith scores, additional Disciplines, Traits presented in later books, etc.). Stick 'em here.

• The Weakness entry is included so you can jot down your character's clan weakness.

• Rituals are special abilities studied under the auspices of Thaumaturgy and Necromancy. If you don't have either of these Disciplines, leave this space blank, or use it for something more appropriate.

• The Blood Bonds section also covers vinculi, which are the special "threads" of sanguinary loyalty possessed by vampires of the Sabbat. For more details on the vinculum and the Vaulderie that creates it, see the **Guide to the Sabbat**.

• The Coterie Chart is a fine place to jot down notes on your troupe's coterie, or to create a "family tree" of coterie relationships.

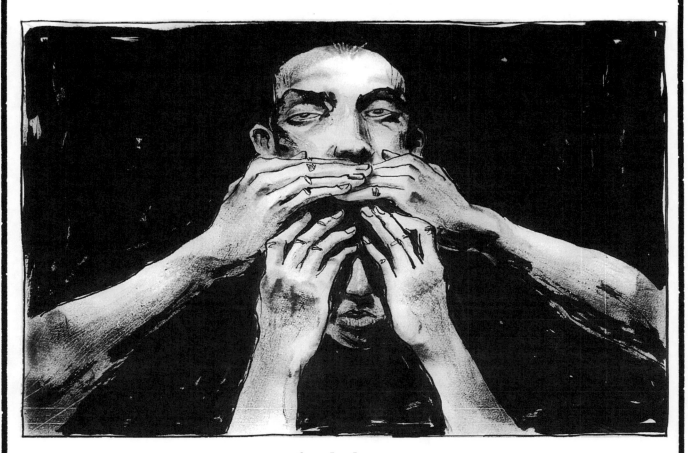

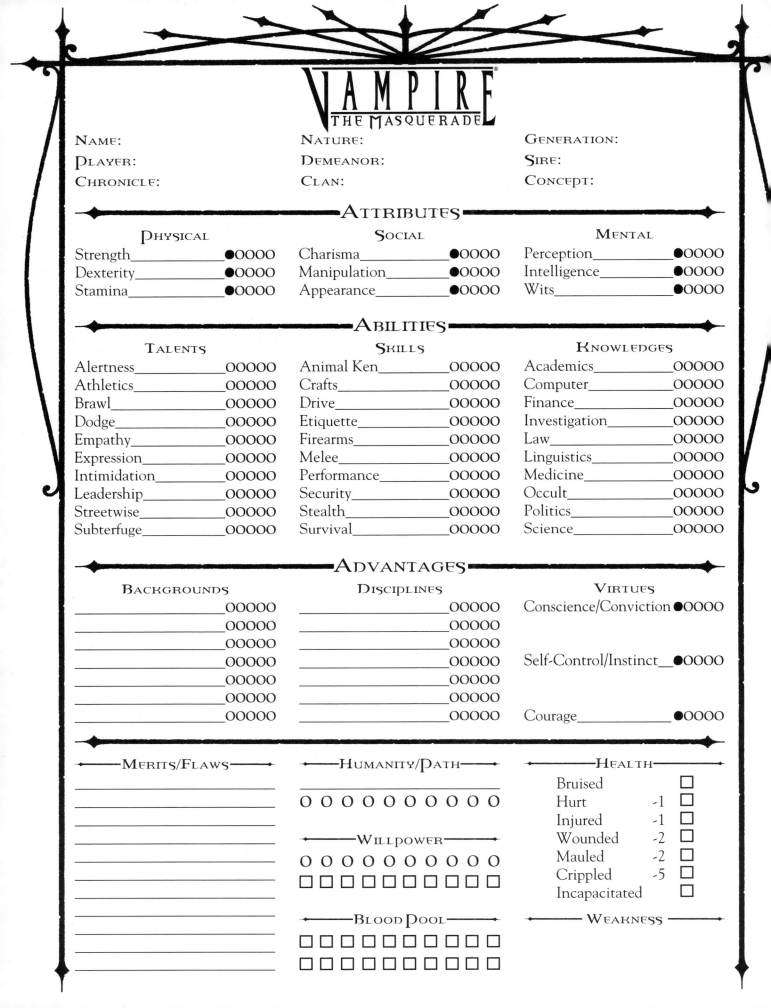

VAMPIRE
THE MASQUERADE

NAME: NATURE: GENERATION:

PLAYER: DEMEANOR: SIRE:

CHRONICLE: CLAN: CONCEPT:

ATTRIBUTES

PHYSICAL
Strength_____ ●OOOO
Dexterity_____ ●OOOO
Stamina_____ ●OOOO

SOCIAL
Charisma_____ ●OOOO
Manipulation_____ ●OOOO
Appearance_____ ●OOOO

MENTAL
Perception_____ ●OOOO
Intelligence_____ ●OOOO
Wits_____ ●OOOO

ABILITIES

TALENTS
Alertness_____ OOOOO
Athletics_____ OOOOO
Brawl_____ OOOOO
Dodge_____ OOOOO
Empathy_____ OOOOO
Expression_____ OOOOO
Intimidation_____ OOOOO
Leadership_____ OOOOO
Streetwise_____ OOOOO
Subterfuge_____ OOOOO

SKILLS
Animal Ken_____ OOOOO
Crafts_____ OOOOO
Drive_____ OOOOO
Etiquette_____ OOOOO
Firearms_____ OOOOO
Melee_____ OOOOO
Performance_____ OOOOO
Security_____ OOOOO
Stealth_____ OOOOO
Survival_____ OOOOO

KNOWLEDGES
Academics_____ OOOOO
Computer_____ OOOOO
Finance_____ OOOOO
Investigation_____ OOOOO
Law_____ OOOOO
Linguistics_____ OOOOO
Medicine_____ OOOOO
Occult_____ OOOOO
Politics_____ OOOOO
Science_____ OOOOO

ADVANTAGES

BACKGROUNDS
_____ OOOOO
_____ OOOOO
_____ OOOOO
_____ OOOOO
_____ OOOOO
_____ OOOOO
_____ OOOOO

DISCIPLINES
_____ OOOOO
_____ OOOOO
_____ OOOOO
_____ OOOOO
_____ OOOOO
_____ OOOOO
_____ OOOOO

VIRTUES
Conscience/Conviction ●OOOO

Self-Control/Instinct__ ●OOOO

Courage_____ ●OOOO

MERITS/FLAWS
_____
_____
_____
_____
_____
_____
_____

HUMANITY/PATH
_____
O O O O O O O O O O

WILLPOWER
O O O O O O O O O O
☐ ☐ ☐ ☐ ☐ ☐ ☐ ☐ ☐ ☐

BLOOD POOL
☐ ☐ ☐ ☐ ☐ ☐ ☐ ☐ ☐ ☐
☐ ☐ ☐ ☐ ☐ ☐ ☐ ☐ ☐ ☐

HEALTH
Bruised   ☐
Hurt   -1   ☐
Injured   -1   ☐
Wounded   -2   ☐
Mauled   -2   ☐
Crippled   -5   ☐
Incapacitated   ☐

WEAKNESS

VAMPIRE
THE MASQUERADE

OTHER TRAITS

_____ OOOOO	_____ OOOOO	_____ OOOOO
_____ OOOOO	_____ OOOOO	_____ OOOOO
_____ OOOOO	_____ OOOOO	_____ OOOOO
_____ OOOOO	_____ OOOOO	_____ OOOOO
_____ OOOOO	_____ OOOOO	_____ OOOOO
_____ OOOOO	_____ OOOOO	_____ OOOOO
_____ OOOOO	_____ OOOOO	_____ OOOOO

RITUALS

NAME	LEVEL
_____	_____
_____	_____
_____	
_____	
_____	
_____	
_____	
_____	
_____	
_____	
_____	
_____	
_____	
_____	
_____	
_____	
_____	
_____	
_____	

EXPERIENCE

TOTAL: _____

TOTAL SPENT: _____

spent on:

_____
_____
_____
_____
_____

DERANGEMENTS

_____
_____
_____
_____
_____
_____
_____

BLOOD BONDS/ VINCULI

BOUND TO	RATING	BOUND TO	RATING
_____	_____	_____	_____
_____	_____	_____	_____
_____	_____	_____	_____
_____	_____	_____	_____

COMBAT

WEAPON	DAMAGE	RANGE	RATE	CLIP	CONCEAL	ARMOR
						_____
						_____
						_____
						_____

VAMPIRE
THE MASQUERADE

EXPANDED BACKGROUND

ALLIES

_____
_____
_____
_____
_____

CONTACTS

_____
_____
_____
_____
_____

FAME

_____
_____
_____
_____
_____

HERD

_____
_____
_____
_____
_____

INFLUENCE

_____
_____
_____
_____
_____

MENTOR

_____
_____
_____
_____
_____

RESOURCES

_____
_____
_____
_____
_____

RETAINERS

_____
_____
_____
_____
_____

STATUS

_____
_____
_____
_____
_____

OTHER

_____
_____
_____
_____
_____

POSSESSIONS

GEAR (CARRIED)

_____
_____
_____
_____
_____

FEEDING GROUNDS

_____
_____
_____
_____

EQUIPMENT (OWNED)

_____
_____
_____
_____
_____

VEHICLES

_____
_____
_____
_____

HAVENS

LOCATION

_____
_____
_____

DESCRIPTION

_____
_____
_____

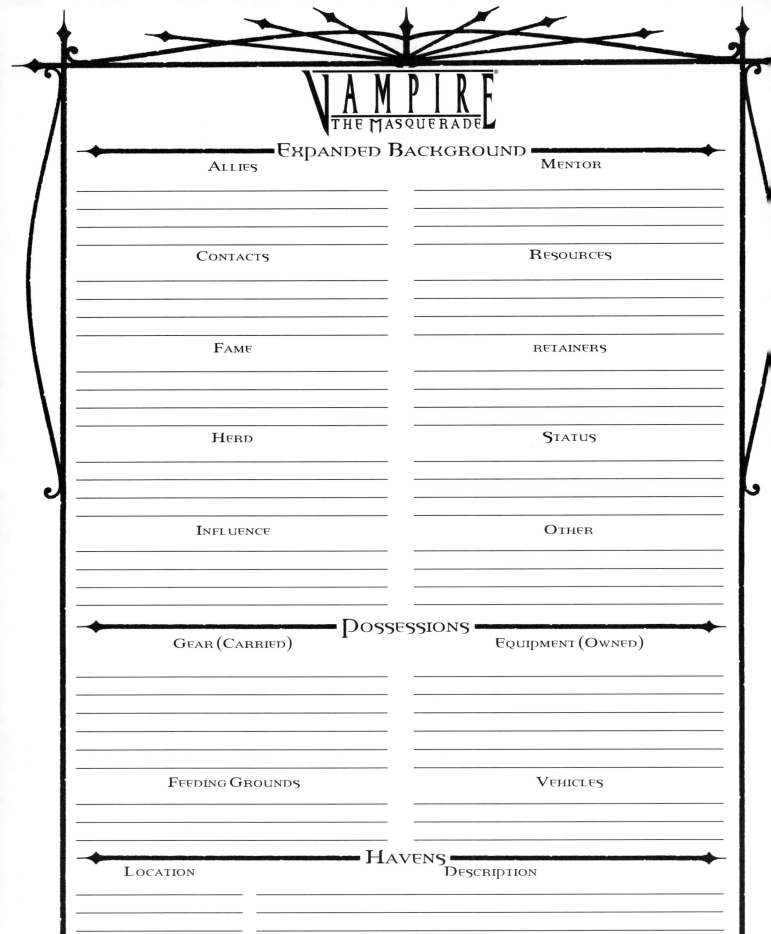

VAMPIRE
THE MASQUERADE

HISTORY
Prelude

_____
_____
_____
_____
_____
_____
_____
_____
_____
_____
_____
_____

APPEARANCE

AGE_____   _____
APPARENT AGE_____   _____
DATE OF BRITH_____   _____
RIP_____   _____
HAIR_____   _____
EYES_____   _____
RACE_____   _____
NATIONALITY_____   _____
HEIGHT_____   _____
WEIGHT_____   _____
SEX_____   _____

VISUALS

COTERIE CHART   CHARACTER SKETCH

Year of the Reckoning

Seven volumes of righteous fury in 1999.

WORLD OF DARKNESS

February	March	July	August	August	October	NOVEMBER
The Fools Luck: The Way of the Commoner	The Cainite Heresy	The Time of Thin Blood	Rage Across the Heavens	Technocracy: The Players Guide	The Ends of Empire	THERE WILL COME A RECKONING.

White Wolf Game Studio